VOYAGE OF THE TRIGON

ADRIANA DeBOLT

CAROUSEL SCIENCE FICTIONS
are published by
AMERICAN ART ENTERPRISES, INC.
12011 Sherman Road
North Hollywood, CA 91605

Voyage of the Trigon

CHAPTER ONE

The presentation was over.

The Vazecry of Kahilur, Jarun Faralum, the insignia of his nobility strung round his neck on a chain of golden asterisks, talked with His High Commander of Kyrale, Emperor of Kam, Filar, and Ming, Faceen of Warlo-IV and Kinto-VI, King of the Xxl Solar Worlds.

"I would have thought, Jarun, after your long absence from us that you would have been desirous of staying put for a while to enjoy your recent accolades," The High Commander said, sipping amber-tyine from a vee-shaped crystal. "But, what should I see upon my desk this morning but a request for permission to go rocketing off on this latest venture."

In fact, The High Commander wasn't as put off as he might have seemed, in that he always felt safer when Jarun was off somewhere else. The wealth of Jarun Faralum, second only to the wealth of The High Commander within the whole Kyralean Empire, was enormous. Of an old and proud Kyralean family, rulers when The High Commander's people were prowling the wilds of Delta-T, Jarun was also extremely popular with the masses. In fact, the tales which had arisen around his exploits and conquests had rather made Jarun a legend in his own time.

Was it any wonder, therefore, that The High Commander always felt a little uncomfortable when the handsome Jarun returned? Was it any wonder that The High Commander was fearful that any extensive stay of Jarun on his home planet would possibly cause eventual friction? Friction being something The High Commander certainly didn't need. In an eventual showdown, The High Commander couldn't be sure Jarun's popularity wouldn't have seen even The High Commander's Elite Corps swinging loyalty toward Jarun.

Not that Jarun had ever shown any indication he was out to glean more power than he already had. In fact, it was his obvious disregard for the subject politic which had kept him as friendly with The High Commander as he was.

If he wasn't driven by a need to achieve power, he certainly wasn't motivated by a need to acquire wealth. His family had been rich before Jarun had ever cracked the labo-vat crystal and emerged into living. The fortune Jarun had since acquired would have supported whole worlds for virtual tirem, let alone support one man who had never bothered to marry (although, the bastards he had fathered were legion).

Jarun was obviously a man of peculiar needs, needs not satisfied long within the civilized environs of home and Empire. His tastes leaned more toward exotic primitive, beyond the limited boundaries established even by the liberal standards of Kyralean society. In fact, were it not for his position and wealth, he might well have been branded a deviate and dealt with accordingly. However, one did not easily label as deviate a man who had heaped such riches on the Empire. And, if his treatment of the barbarians he encountered in deep space was less humanitarian than it might have been, well, allowances had to be made, didn't they? After all, who could much care what went on in conquests of primitive worlds as long as spacecraft continued to return laden with the wealth of these conquered pockets of space?

"I seem to be happiest in deep space," Jarun admitted, "away from the trappings of pomp and circumstance."

Yes, The High Commander didn't doubt that. In deep space, Jarun controlled a little world of his own, didn't he? Surrounded by his own cohort of loyal men, he was free to exercise certain rights of command, do certain things, satisfy certain wants that would have been condemned were they brought in from the distant vacuums.

The High Commander had his reports. He had his spies among Jarun's crew. Although calling them spies was really something of a misnomer, in that The High Commander suspected Jarun read everything before it was passed on to The High Commander. Not that Jarun had apparently censored the material. Jarun rightly suspected that his conduct beyond the Kyralean Boundaries was hardly liable to reprimand.

The paperwork to pass across The High Commander's desk bespoke certain horrors that would have been considered atrocities if committed nearer. As it stood, however, any Empire Counsel called to sit in judgment would have hardly concerned themselves. And, Jarun's position was of such import that too many fortunes of those members on the Empire Counsel had been built upon Jarun's spoils of conquest.

"I'm a little loath to let you go," The High Commander said, "especially on a project such as this one that has already seen two ExploraStarShips lost without a trace. If the fabled Cities of Zythin do exist, evidence would seem to indicate they aren't unable to handle those who come to sack them of their legendary treasures."

"Reports have the planet in the Klyko System,"

Jarun said. "Has any evidence come from that region of lifeforms of even medium intelligence?"

"No, but the area remains mainly unexplored, doesn't it?" The High Commander reminded. "Who knows what lies just beyond the void? Considering the kind and number of spacecraft that have mysteriously disappeared when even drawn near to that area, I would be inclined to believe there might be intelligence there that hasn't yet met the eye."

"Perhaps so," Jarun admitted. "On the other hand, maybe it's merely just such a challenge that I find so exciting."

"The idea of sacking the Yunilic Planetoids no longer catches your fancy?" The High Commander asked. "It was my impression, before your last exit from us, that the Yunilic Planetoids were next on your list. There's certainly more information to verify the presence of treasure there than in the Klyko System."

"Let Jackson take on the Yunilic Planetoids," Juran said. "He's been out to gain access to them for tirem."

"Held back, I might add, only by your options on the area."

"I shall charge him for the privilege, of course," Jarun said. "Splitting profits, of course, with the Crown."

"We've never questioned your generosity," The High Commander said, feeling the rhythmic waves of heat, spawned by the amber-tyine he was drinking, undulating through his body.

Jarun's glance took in the milling crowd come to do homage to the man whose spaceships had so recently returned from far Toptl filled to the brim with treasures coveted as well by the civilized Kyraleans as by the primitives who had previously owned them.

"Spot anyone of interest in the crowd?" The High Commander asked, a faint smile playing across his thin lips.

"Interesting?" Jarun replied, as if the question had somehow struck him as odd.

"There isn't a woman (a man, either, for that matter) in this whole crowded room who wouldn't be more than delighted to join you afterwards, if you but indicated interest."

"Oh, *that* kind of interest!" Jarun said, giving a small laugh.

"You're obviously ready for such relaxation, I would imagine," The High Commander said, his statement attempting to mask a knowledge that few people in the room would have really been so willing to indulge Jarun's sexual fantasies if, in fact, they were to learn what they were. "After all, you were a long time away from the creature comforts, were you not?"

"I suspect the drives to which you refer no longer burn so hot inside of me as they once did at a younger age," Jarun said. If he knew The High Commander knew what kind of flames did burn in their stead, he didn't let on.

"You're hardly an old man," The High Commander

reminded.

In fact, Jarun, at one-hundred tirem looked nowhere near that age. He still had the face and body of a young man. In fact, it was rumored he had sampled Dilna Water with the Queen of Korfu before the cataclysm of Baboc-IV disintegrated four planets in the Mimul System, Korfu being one.

Yes, Jarun was in fine physical condition. No one looking would have guessed that The High Commander was the younger of the two. Possibly because age had never been kind to The High Commander. Not only that, but he had never been very handsome to begin with. Certainly not handsome enough so that the Queen of Korfu would have shared secrets with him for a sampling of his sexual prowess.

The High Commander was five-ten. He was slight of build, having been a sickly child. Those same childhood diseases had taken most of his hair and hadn't given it back. What little was left of his hair, colored orange in the unattractive hue of a mento-melon, was now covered by the official coronet.

His eyes were large, his pupils black. His eyebrows and eyelashes were light to the point of seeming nonexistent without application of artificial coloring.

His mouth was too thin.

Jarun, on the other hand, was six-feet-two, in his bare feet, raised an inch higher by his boots.

His hair was jet black, arranged in a skillful tousle that had men and women alike fantasizing the run of

13

their fingers through it.

His eyes were purple. Kyralean purple, giving proof positive that he could trace his ancestry back to The First High Commander, Mumeptic Cru. His eyebrows were well-defined, his eyelashes were lush and sooty.

His mouth was full and sensuous.

His skin was naturally dark, having just the exact shade of pigment that everyone spent hours in the tansom rooms trying so desperately (and usually unsuccessfully) to duplicate.

He looked all attractive innocence, when (as The High Commander well knew) innocent was the last adjective that could have truthfully been applied to Jarun Faralum.

How had Jarun managed to maintain a façade of innocence when he had dropped so far into the darker areas of experience? While the High Commander, whose experiences were relatively tame by comparison, looked as if he had aged far beyond his time? If The High Commander hadn't known better, he might have suspected he had been caused to show the effects of each new perversion Jarun indulged beyond the authority of civilized worlds.

"Have you stumbled upon any new indications that there really are any Cities of Zythin?" The High Commander asked, deciding to keep his jealousy under control.

And, it was just jealousy, wasn't it? Pure and simple.

"A Nordoic freighter, drifting without power, was fired upon and destroyed in Scalic Area III," Jarun said.

"Oh?" The High Commander responded. "Fired upon by whom?"

It wasn't all that unusual that he hadn't heard of the attack. The High Commander governed an Empire that extended to over five-thousand systems. If the destruction of one Nordoic freighter hadn't been relayed to his ears, it had obviously been relayed to the people who took care of such things.

"Enemy unknown," Jarun said. "However, other similar destructs in that particular area would tend to indicate someone is hiding something, wouldn't you agree?"

"I could probably give you any number of conflicting explanations," The High Commander said. "But, why spoil your fun?"

"You will give me permission, then, to launch the proposed expedition?" Jarun asked.

"We'll see," The High Commander said. "There really can't be any chance of you leaving us immediately anyway. My subjects would never forgive me were I to allow you to slip away so soon after your arrival."

But, yes, The High Commander would let him go, wouldn't he? The High Commander simply felt too uncomfortable with the electricity the presence of Jarun Faralum seemed to release within any room that man entered.

CHAPTER TWO

Jarun stood on the balcony, leaning on the parapet.

The city was still in celebration. Lights were burning. Lazo-fires were flaming large along the horizon. Faint streams of music wafted on the nonexistent breeze. Distant laughter was echoed by other revelers celebrating the return of Jarun Faralum.

Five ExploraStarShips had gone with him to far Toptl. He had returned with three, each with a cargo of booty that would have purchased the Empire a whole fleet of the large ExploraStarShips.

He had been back three days. Already he was anxious to head out again.

He found the city stifling. He found the opulence of

the Palace less preferable than the somewhat austere quarters on his spacecraft.

He wouldn't have come back at all if he hadn't found it necessary to dump the cargo of accumulated wealth. He certainly couldn't stop off just anywhere and unload a fortune.

So, he had brought it back to the city. Just as he had always brought it back to the city. Because, it was all of little use to him elsewhere. He had more than enough money to live out the rest of his life as comfortably as The High Commander himself. Besides, the money paid here bought him the backing and stamp of approval of the Kyralean Empire, which was no mean purchase, considering the influence of the Empire within the Galaxy. As an official ambassador, Jarun's expeditions took on a clout they wouldn't have had were he to have launched such expeditions on his own. And, launch them on his own, he would have been able to do, too, if he hadn't minded going out without the guise of diplomatic officiality.

The vis-button sounded, signaling someone at the door. He turned from the balcony, crossing into the lush accommodations of his suite.

His serva-boy had already seen who it was, appearing suddenly with an attractive young woman.

"Sorry to disturb you, sir," the serva-boy said, "but, the young lady comes from The High Commander."

"It's all right," Jarun said magnanimously, although the "gift" (for gift it most assuredly was)

17

wasn't exactly what Jarun had had in mind for the evening.

"My name is Malina," the young woman said, flashing a smile that showed milky white teeth. She shook her attractive name of blonde hair so that it framed her oval face in cascades of silky curls.

Her eyes were pale gold, possibly denoting a lineage traceable to a Keanterbind influence, or maybe even Dantiloian.

Her lips were full, made glossy by a peach-colored gloss.

She wore a robe of clinging diaphum that was the color of her painted mouth. The robe revealed, in its drapery, a shape which was obviously voluptuous.

The High Commander at least sent the best his stable had to offer.

"The sleep-chamber is that way, Malina," Jarun said, motioning toward a slido-door. "Why don't you go in there and wait for me to join you?"

The girl obediently did as she had been instructed.

Once she was in the sleep-chamber, though, the door closed behind her, she couldn't really know that Jarun was wondering if it were really going to be worth the effort.

He really had no desire to. . .

The viewer screen was activated, flashing blue in signal of an incoming message.

A short time later, Jarun had Bilo Niltak fading in for viewing. It was several moments longer before the

18

audio came in clearly.

"Sorry to interrupt you during your celebrations, sir," Bilo said. His official rank was Sub-Commander-First-Grade, one of the men Jarun had had with him for tirem and trusted. "But, you requested a report on anything we might turn up here."

"The interruption was welcome," Jarun said. "Actually, I'm already beginning to go a little stir crazy around here. I envy you being where you are."

Where Bilo was exactly was in a Lyro-pod, circling Disnom-II in the Klyko System. He and a contingent of Jarun's men had been sent there, independent of the ExploraStarShips which had returned to Kyrale with the booty of far Toptl.

Bilo's mission had been to survey the lifeforms in residence on several planets in the System, scanning for possible mental references to the fabled Cities of Zythin.

The Cities, long a part of Galactic mythology, were supposedly all located on one planet, somewhere in the Galaxy, and contained fortunes beyond belief. References to the Cities on at least four different planets, in three different planet systems, had seemed to indicate, as with many tales of folklore, that there was something to the story.

The story being that Kiru-Tos, a mighty Wiseman on long-destroyed Zythin, did successfully predict the cataclysm which was destined to destroy his world. The Wiseman and his followers, therefore, had packed up all of their substantial wealth and had fled in a space flotilla to some distant world thought safe from catastrophe. Wherein they constructed ten cities of superlative beauty.

However, as the legend went, the people of Zythin weren't really compatible with their new environment and, in a period of several tirem, completely died out, leaving behind them their undecaying fortunes.

ExplorShips had been searching for these fabled Cities of Zythin since David Moroctin set out on his explorations in the 9th Duric, C.C.

"We've snatched a Kafir here," Billo said. "We're taking elimination into its final stages."

"But, you've come up with something, yes?"

"Visitors," Bilo replied. "They apparently sat down here before the primitives were living in caves. There are paintings now existing within some of the deeper religio-caves. Mind-readout turned up depictions of representations similar to the descriptions of Myron Dedal in his *Discourses on Civilizations in Flux.*"

Myron Dedal was a chronolographer from Coolx-2, a planet in the Datr System. His work was uncovered in the 14th Duric by Archeo-scientist Faro Deese who discovered and excavated the ruins of a nation which had apparently ceased when its star went into fade. Myron supposedly recorded mention of a stopover by the Wiseman of Zythin some four-hundred tirem before Myron had been born. Myron told of how the early ruler of Coolx-2 had been transported aboard one

20

Zythinean spacecraft and had marveled at the riches he had beheld there.

It was Myron who had described the Zythineans as being "large of body; covered from head to foot with long, silky hair (male and female alike); having three massive arms, two of which were walked upon like legs; having three eyes and two noses; who conversed via sound vibrations passed on by touching."

It was Myron who had recorded the demise of the Zythineans once they had settled their ten cities. Although, a missing section of his metat-scroll apparently held all references as to how Myron had chanced upon that bit of information on Coolx-2.

In fact, it was the lack of explanation for Myron's tale of Zythinean destruction within an alien environment which left many scholars assuming his whole story was nothing more than a fabrication: a Coolxian fairy tale.

However, over the tirem, references to Zythinean creatures having touched down elsewhere in the Galaxy tended to support Myron's story, at least as far as the existence of such creatures went.

And, the Zythos of Planet Mortar had folk legends that went so far as to say their ancestors were deposited where they were when a contingent broke away from a Mothership of some remnants of a civilization fleeing such a cataclysm as that which had apparently happened on Zythin. The Zythos not only having a name-designate similar to that of the fabled

Zythineans but having a very similar body makeup, which natural selection could be argued to have mutated for better adaption to the Planet Mortar. They having six lungs to filter the smoke-ridden air, webbing on their feet (two legs not three) to better navigate a planet almost totally consumed by vegabogs, and hooded eye membranes (once again conceivably mutated as a protection from the constant particles afloat in the air); but, also, having a hair-covered body, three eyes, two noses, and the ability to converse via thought vibrations conveyed by touching.

"Will you play me the Kafir's mind-readout?" Jarun requested of Bilo.

A mind-readout leeched information from the victim's brain, reconverting to mental images on video screens. It was much used for interrogation during the Fin-Frx Wars but had since been pretty much phased out because of the detrimental effects of causing scar tissue to form on the victim's brain, the likes of which eventually resulted in the victim's insanity. The Empire Council, therefore, authorized the mind-readout only on the most primitive of lifeforms, finding it too inhumane to subject civilized varieties to such torment as accompanied and followed the utilization.

Not that Jarun had ever paid that much attention to the Empire Council. In fact, it could well have been successfully argued that a Disnom-II Kafir was already several steps above the intelligence level which

22

made the mind-readout outlaw. The Kafirs of Disnom-II had actually progressed to the point of devising their own writing, if based on a simple, ten-letter, tonal alphabet. They dwelt in communal caves and were hardly considered war-like.

What they were considered, however, was secretive, especially as regarded their religious ceremonies and customs which were rumored to be conducted ten times an orbit within a series of caves and tunnels, some as far as a mega-mile beneath the planet surface. Three religio-scientists had attempted to research the Disnom-II religious doctrines, one having lived among the Kafirs for one-hundred tirem before giving up his project as a hopeless undertaking, what with the lack of Kafir cooperation.

If Jarun, therefore, wanted access to Kafir secrets, a mind-readout seemed by far the easiest and most direct conduit.

That he had specifically requested Bilo to snatch a religious man for the interrogation was because visitors from other planets, when setting down on primitive worlds, were invariably mistaken for deities and, thus, worshiped as such. If, therefore, the Zythineans had set down on Disnom-II, it was more than conceivable that the incident was recorded and held secure within local religious dogma which (especially in the case of the secretive Kafir) was often held too sacred for uninitiated ears.

Which indeed did tend to be the case, as proven by

the results of Bilo's interrogation of the Kafir.

The mind-readout Bilo relayed on the view screen for Jarun's viewing was obviously a segment from some past religious ceremony the Kafir had attended.

What Jarun saw was basically what the Kafir had once seen and registered on brain impulses now leeched by a machine.

From what Jarun could tell, he was progressing slowly through a dark passageway, the flickering lights, perhaps, indicating the way was being lit by torches. Which seemed a logical explanation, considering the Kafir penchant for caves and cave-dwelling.

Jarun was on the point of asking for a speedup of the readout when the tunnel suddenly blossomed out into a small chamber. At that moment, the picture was locked in by Bilo on the other end.

"Notice the far wall," Bilo said by way of pointing out a series of distant cave paintings. "I'll bring the pertinent one in for magnification."

Several flashes of the viewer screen brought the distant paintings into sharper focus. One of them was obviously of a creature having three arms, two having hands planted on a flat plain, the third hand reaching upward for a star painted about two feet above it.

It was depicted as being covered with vertical, stick-like lines which might well have been stylized renditioning of hair. Within the vertical scratch were three horizontal notches. Noses?

"How does the Kafir identify?" Jarun asked.

"Stand by for computer audio conversions," Bilo said.

The visual remaining static (the cave picture somewhere within the bowels of Disnom-II), the computer audio consisted of a verbal renditioning of Bilo's questioning of the Kafir, the Kafir touch tones having been converted into Kyralean speech pattern.

"I'm interested in the pictures on the wall," Bilo was heard saying. "Why don't you tell me about them."

"The ball is the early formation of existence from the void," the Kafir was heard to reply, the computer rendering such translation in a voice that was neuter in form and inflection. "The cube is the void from which the ball. . ."

"More specifically, I want to know about the painting to the right," Bilo said. "See the hairy creature with the three arms?"

A lengthy pause followed, interrupted by Bilo's voice.

"Tell me about the three-armed creature."

"It is evil," the computer translated from the Kafir original.

"Evil?"

"It is evil," the Kafir repeated.

"It has a name?"

"Eater of Kafir," the Kafir replied.

"Eater of Kafir?" Bilo quizzed.

"Dropped from the sky," the Kafir replied. "A

plague in the days before Kafir knew caves. A plague that drove us into the ground to escape."

"Zythineans?" Bilo queried.

"Hungry," the Kafir replied. "Came to fetch Kafir for his pot."

"Come from where?" Bilo asked.

"From cocoons that hung in the sky," the Kafir replied.

"To eat Kafir?"

"To eat and leave. Sacrifice to Thin, lest he return to eat your children and your children's children!"

"Thin?"

"To utter that name is the tantan to conjure him up again."

"Conjure him up from where?"

"Ten temples in the sky."

"Where in the sky?"

"I do not know. Nobody knows but Thin."

"Why ten temples?"

"Ten temples from ten cocoons. He came like a spider to snare us in his sticky web. To feast on us like a fila-bird on newhatched chreeks. We sacrifice on each ten pilos that he may be satisfied and not return."

"Sacrifice?"

"Thin was an eater of Kafir."

"Yes."

There was a resulting click as the recorder was switched off. When Bilo next spoke, it was obviously at the moment and not from the previously heard recording.

"There's more, but it's relatively uninteresting. The sacrifices, needless to say, were of Kafir by Kafir."

"Wouldn't the religio-scientists be delighted to hear that?" Jarun commented wryly. He had no intentions of telling them. They would undoubtedly have been more appalled by the utilization of the mind-readout for gleaning the information than in any insight to Kafir religion which the data might have given them.

"A projection from supposed touchdowns on Kimpol-IV, Disop, Coolx-2, and Disnom-II would point toward Scalic Area III, correct?" Bilo asked.

"Unless that was point of origin," Jarun said. "In which case the Zythinean point of colonization might be in the opposite direction. Except, of course, that it seems highly unlikely they would have been scrounging for food at their trip beginning, now does it?"

"Shall I proceed on to Tibur-I and take another sampling from there?"

"Proceed immediately," Jarun instructed. "By then, I shall have hopefully cleared up the paperwork here to be ready to join you with a charter from The High Commander."

"He was favorable to the project then?"

"Favorable on two counts," Jarun said. "One, because he always welcomes the prospect of a new fortune to fill his coffers. Two, because he always feels safer when I'm out of sight. The place is no less full of intrigue than when we left it. Perhaps, it's even more glutted. I've heard The High Commander was nearly assassinated before our arrival. The Georgian Faction again."

"I don't envy you within the mire," Bilo said. "May I wish you much speed in your removal?"

"Which will be as quickly achieved as I can manage it. Now, about the Kafir."

"We have him on hold, programmed for destruct. You said to relay the termination procedure."

"I only wish I were there."

"Computer has indicated an injection of *tyllino-frescunium-D,*" Bilo said. "Shall I tender possible alternatives?"

"No, terminate as computer has designated," Jarun instructed.

He settled back, feeling the excitement tingling throughout his body as the screen image was switched to a viewing of the Kafir in the interrogation chair.

The Kafir was a primitive of the humanoid variety, subspecies *Disnorian cilichis monsterous.* It had two stocky legs, ended each with a ten-toed foot that was decidedly splayed. Its body was compact and so hairy that it was difficult to tell where it left off and the animal fur of its clothing began. Its head was almost as big as its torso, constructed with large projections over the eyesockets and a massively square jawline. Its pupils were large, accustomed as it was to spending a good deal of its time in the dark. Of course, the extent of the present dilation was more a result of the after-effects of the mind-readout.

"We are ready for injection," Bilo informed, heard but unseen.

"Proceed," Jarun said. He was beginning to sweat.

\ * * *

He felt, rather than saw, the slight closing of the slido-door, having not really been aware as to just when the door had been slid open just a crack.

He disengaged the viewer screen and came to his feet, turning to face the sleep-chamber and the woman he knew to be inside it.

He had been so caught up in the death of the Kafir, he had completely forgotten the woman, Malina.

The woman, on the other hand, had obviously not forgotten him. Whether from curiosity, impatience, or an instruction from someone else, she had opened the door and had seen Jarun at the viewer screen. Seeing that, she must have seen what Jarun had seen.

He stood and headed for the sleep-chamber, pausing briefly on the threshhold to convert his lazo-gun from kill to stun. Gun in his right hand, he activated the entro-button and heard the faint sigh of plasto pulling to one side to allow him entrance.

She was naked and in the sleep-cushion, a sheet pulled modestly to her chin while the curves of her body, beneath the draping of the material, were more erotic than merely naked flesh.

When, however, she saw the lazo-gun, she must have suspected that her observations of Jarun at the viewer screen mustn't have gone undetected by him. Because, in total disregard of modesty, she threw back the sheet, coming free of the covers in a move—Jarun supposed—which was intended to get her past him to safety.

"You stupid bitch!" he said, squeezing off the trigger.

Hitting her was like hitting a sitting duck. Actually, it was easier, since she had presented a far larger target.

She went down in a crumpled heap, her limbs sprawled like that of a rag doll tossed on the floor.

Jarun holstered his weapon and went over to the body. Kneeling, he checked the base of her slender neck for a pulse. While his gun had been set for stun, there were some people allergic to the lazo-dosage, no matter how minimal the amount. Those few were known to die immediately.

Malina, however, was obviously one of the vast majority who needed a sizable dosage for kill, because she was still alive.

Jarun scooped her up in his arms and carried her back to the sleep-cushion. He dropped her unceremoniously on top of the sheet.

Looking down on her naked body, he realized she was really quite beautiful.

Though, he channeled his mind into other areas, knowing there would be plenty of time to admire her body and do with it what he may once he had the woman secured so he wouldn't have to risk losing her.

He tied her spreadeagled on the sleep-cushion, using ripped strips from a tiliinth pullover he had in the clothes-storage area.

He then pulled a chair up closer and sat down.

Checking the digital readout on his wristband, he computed about how much longer it would be before Malina began to revive.

His estimate was correct, almost to the minute.

Malina groaned first, swallowed twice, and then tried to roll. The ties, however, kept her from doing the latter.

Her eyelids fluttered, finally coming open to reveal golden irises gone slightly dilated by the lazo-injection.

"What . . . what happened?" she asked, her pinkish tongue dampening the peach-colored gloss smeared over her sensuous lips.

"Seems you had a little accident," Jarun said, more than a little sarcastically. "Seems you ran into a lazo-stun."

Her whole face registered sudden fear, her brain having obviously realized most of what had led up to the present moment.

"Why?" she asked, obviously feeling the best defense was a feigning of complete innocence. Even though, her gut-feeling told her that Jarun Faralum wasn't about to be fooled by her guise.

"Why don't you tell me?" Jarun countered.

"I don't know what you're. . ."

"Please spare me an exercise in theatrics!" Jarun said in interruption. "Since you are here under a pass issued and signed by The High Commander, I must assure that you are here spying under his request, is that not so?"

"Spying?" Malina asked. "I don't know what you're talking about. I naturally panicked when I saw your drawn gun. Who wouldn't have panicked under such circumstances?"

"You're prepared to tell me, then, that you weren't listening to my conversation on the viewer screen?"

"Viewer screen?" Malina asked, shuddering with remembrance of what she had seen, knowing she wasn't fooling Jarun in the least by her denial. "What viewer screen?"

"Be difficult, then," Jarun said, coming to his feet. "But, I would certainly recommend that you think very seriously about volunteering your cooperation. Because, whether you volunteer it or not, I can assure you that I shall have the information I want."

He turned and left the sleep-chamber.

Once back in the living-space, he stopped momentarily to consider what specific accoutrement he was going to need to convince the woman that he did indeed mean business. Back on the ExploraShip, there would have been no problem There was specialized equipment on board designed to make anyone or anything spill his, her, or its guts.

It was highly unlikely, though, that Jarun could have gotten the woman, sight unseen, all of the way to the ship in the docking area. Therefore, his interrogation was going to have to be conducted here. If he were forced into improvising, well, then, improvise was what he would do.

He went to the storage-safe off to one side of the room, opening it with a coded combination and the registering of his handprint on the detecto-plate.

The heavy doors slid to the side, revealing a small sampling of Jarun's share of the treasures sacked from far Toptl.

What he was looking for was some object so foreign to Malina that the woman wouldn't have the vaguest notion for what it was used.

His selection was a Toptl Trance Lamp, so named not because it induced a tranced state but because it was commonly found in the Toptl Trance Dens. Trance Dens being rooms set aside in most Toptl households where the residents could periodically escape to inhale corkonaine vapors from a burner set up specifically for that purpose.

Corkonaine was a derivative of the more powerful hallucinogen *corkoonofis*, the latter obtained from the crushed petals of the Toptl swamp lily. Burning *corkoonofis* had been known to send imbibers tripping for virtual tirem. Corkonaine, however, was a milder version that produced mind-bends of comparatively slight duration and nature.

The Toptl Trance Lamps, when activated, produced a throbbing blue-green glow and a decided low humming that could penetrate flesh and material like a tyurgo massage.

The lamp was just the implement for which Jarun was looking. He removed it from the other treasures in the storage-safe and sealed the safe back up.

He carried the lamp back to the sleep-chamber, entering with lamp in hand.

"And, look what we have here," Jarun said, holding the lamp so the bound Malina would have a good view of it.

"What is it?" Malina asked.

She had obviously been struggling against her ties while Jarun had been gone, because her ankles and wrists wore pinkish bracelets where the cloth had chafed tender flesh.

"A mind-readout machine," Jarun lied. Then, he added, just on the slim chance that Malina had seen the Kyralean variety, "One used by the Toptlians."

"A mind-readout!"

While it was apparent the woman wouldn't have known a mind-readout if she had been hit over the head with one, it was, at least, evident that she had a rough idea of what one was. Whether she had picked up the information in the employ of The High

Commander (or someone else), or if she had merely made certain deductions via her eavesdropping on Jarun's viewer-screen conversation with Bilo, was of little import.

"With this little machine," Jarun said, sitting down, balancing the lamp on his left knee so that Malina wasn't losing out on her view of it, "I shall have every iota of information written on the impulses of your brain, whether you wish to part with them or not. And, when I'm through, I will be far more knowledgeable than I already am, and you will be a vegetable with a brain leeched clean—of everything."

"Mind-readouts have been outlawed by the Empire Council," Malina said, her eyes wide with terror. "You wouldn't dare use one on me within the city boundaries."

"Quite informed, aren't you?" Jarun said, giving a smile full of little or no humor. "The Empire Council Directive on the banning of mind-readouts is still classified as secret. Hardly reading material readily available to a common whore in The High Commander's stable."

Which shut her up soon enough.

Jarun found it hard to believe that The High Commander had sent such an amateur to do the job of a pro. On the other hand, he had seen hardened agents break down at the threat of being subjected to a mind-readout, knowing, as they did, that the machine could wipe their past and present clean with the flick of a switch.

"You're such a beautiful woman," Jarun said. He pushed the activation button on the lamp.

The lamp, with its own inbuilt power source, immediately came to life. It glowed with a dancing blue-green light. The hum of it penetrated the room, faintly erotic for Jarun, more than a little frightening for the woman tied on the sleep-cushion.

"You're also extremely young," Jarun continued. "How young? Thirty tirem? Twenty-five? You've only just begun to live. Yet, it's surprising how much data a brain can store in just that short of a time. All sorts of facts and figures and memories: date of birth, place of birth, father, mother, childhood experiences, etcetera ad infinitum. You know, it is said that a person's character is actually formed within the first four tirem after his birth, formed by the things that have happened around him. Shall I tell you what happens when a brain is suddenly leeched of all that character-contributing data?"

"I had to come here!" Malina said. Her neck tendons were taut, causing her voice to come out obviously strained. "When The High Commander issues a direct order, it is impossible not to obey."

"You were sent by The High Commander, then?" Jarun said, leaving the lamp activated. He could see where the lamp might well have offered additional stimulus for a Toptlian tripping. Even without the benefit of corkonaine, the pulsing light bestowed its

36

own surrelism to the room.

"Yes," Malina admitted, not willing to sacrifice her mind-images just because she was an unwitting pawn in some power game The High Commander was playing.

"Why?"

"He wanted you watched," Malina said. "And, figuring the scandal would have been too greatly put against him if it were discovered he had bugged your suite of rooms, he sent me to report on what mechanical spy devices couldn't be used to do."

"But, why would he want me watched?" Jarun asked, although he already knew the answer.

Malina knew he knew the answer and told him as much.

"Yes, I suppose you're right," Jarun admitted with a sigh.

What a fool The High Commander was, thinking Jarun could possibly be concerned with the power inherent in supreme command of an empire. What Jarun wanted out of life couldn't possibly be found within the narrow confines of existence in which a High Commander was forced to reign. Jarun would have thought The High Commander would have recognized that fact a long time ago. As a matter of fact, it had been with the express hope of educating The High Commander to that fact that Jarun had allowed so many uncensored reports on Jarun's activities in deep space to filter back to the High

Commander's desk. However, a man motivated by one type of power was obviously hard-pressed to believe all men weren't motivated by that same calling, thus, making the High Commander still suspect of Jarun's intentions.

Not that Jarun wouldn't have more actively sought out the supreme coronet (he rightly figuring that it was in his power to put up a better showing than anybody else to wrench the ruler's diadem from the present incompetent in reign) if The High Commander really was given carte blanche to do what and when he pleased. But, that wasn't really the case, was it? Gone were the days when The High Commander was one step below God (sometimes designated a god himself)—whomever that god happened to be at the moment. In the present day and age, there were too many factions firmly entrenched, those factions able to keep even The High Commander in check. The High Commander, whether consciously aware of it or not, had to continually live in fear that what he was doing one day might cause friction among one or more factions the next day, a uniting of factions quite possibly forming a power-bond strong enough to usurp the throne.

The present wearer of the Kyralean coronet certainly couldn't rest easy, knowing his own ancestor, Babic Nylecton had been the head of just such a faction which had successfully launched a frontal attack that had toppled the Jeulisic line of Kyralean Emperors.

Jarun, as a High Commander, certainly wouldn't have been allowed the amusements he found in deep space. Nor would he have been able to introduce such amusements into the civilized Kyralean network. His needs, he had long ago recognized, were not of the present age of watered-down desires and impulses. And if, in the majority of his crew, he had found men who were equally inclined toward needs more basic and primeval than the present milksop needs held by the majority of the Empire, he and his men were certainly not numbered nearly enough to be able to force such deviate mores upon whole societies that would have been appalled at even the mere suspicions of them.

No, Jarun didn't want to be a High Commander. What he wanted, he now had—or, would once again have as soon as he was out of this place and among primitive nations wherein his word was really law.

"The High Commander fears the Georgian Faction is out to make you King," Malina said, made uneasy by Jarun's long stretch of contemplative silence. "They tried an assassination attempt just prior to your scheduled arrival which, if successful, would have seen them offering you the crown immediately upon your disembarkation of your spacecraft."

"And, The High Commander seriously thinks I was part of such a conspiracy?"

"Had he thought that, I doubt you would be here," Malina said.

"Unless, of course, he feared the repercussions of

killing a national hero, proof or no proof of attempted regicide," Jarun said.

"Not even a national hero is above the law," Malina said.

Jarun laughed, thinking that the sooner he got away from this cesspool of intrigue, the better it would be. If The High Commander really thought Jarun were involved in the Georgian Conspiracy, Jarun's life was definitely in danger. Not that The High Commander would have him killed in any manner that could be traced back to the throne; but, The High Commander *would* have Jarun killed.

Jarun snapped off the Toptl Trance Lamp. He wouldn't be needing the false threat it offered to Malina any more.

He stood, carrying the lamp off to a storage-cabinet to one side of the room. He placed it on the cabinet and began to undress.

When he was finished, he turned back to the cabinet, kneeling to take a long metalic shaft from the bottom drawer. When he stood, he held the shaft gripped tightly within his right hand.

The look in his eye must have told Malina more than she wanted to know.

"What are you going to do?" she asked, her voice sticking in her throat. She tugged at the bindings holding her wrists and ankles, no more successful in escape this time than she had been the last time she had made the attempt.

CHAPTER THREE

"I'm afraid not," Deil Magnor said.

Deil was in charge of troop assignment and reassignment aboard Empire spacecraft.

"There has to be someone available," Captain-Major Coughlin Mowler insisted.

"To your and your General's specifications?" Deil replied with a small laugh. "I'm afraid not. And, believe me, I have been keeping my eyes open."

"General Faralum isn't going to like this," Coughlin informed. He didn't much like it himself. He had been charged with refilling quotas for the latest expedition, and he was already up against an apparent roadblock.

"He would be even less pleased if I were to send him someone who wouldn't . . . shall we say? . . . fit in."

"I can't believe there isn't someone available here," Coughlin insisted, once again shuffling through the computa-folders.

"There's the possibility of potential showing up in one of the colonial schools," Deil said, trying to sound encouraging. He, as much as Coughlin, wished there were a communications officer available to fit the bill. General Faralum had been exceedingly generous to Deil in the past for channeling the "right" kind of men in his direction. However, Deil wasn't about to risk the potential consequences of giving General Faralum the wrong man. And, from the computa-data-readouts on psychological diagnosis and evaluation, Deil had little doubt but that there was no one presently available as a likely candidate for the key position of communications officer on one of the ExploraStarShips under General Faralum's command.

"When will you know if there's anyone qualified in the colonial schools?" Coughlin asked, already figuring he knew the answer.

"As soon as there's time for them to get me the information I've requested on my queries," Deil replied.

Even if there was potential, the time lost in sending for it, and then having it arrive before the expedition's projected embarkation, made it presently worthless.

"What about this one?" Coughlin asked, pulling out one computa-file and tossing it across the table to Deil.

Deil checked out the coded name on the identification flap without bothering to pick up the folder. He knew the contents of most files without having to open them.

If Coughlin thought Deil hadn't spent a good deal of time thoroughly going over the files, he was sadly mistaken. Deil knew most of the information by heart. The data in the file of Lieutenant Renson Carlylean was no exception.

"Yes, I can see where you might be interested in Renson Carlylean," Deil said. "He graduated at the top of his class. His brilliancy in the field is unquestioned. However, you and I both know that the psychological profiles of the officers of a crew under General Faralum are something a bit special. I'm not sure Renson meets such qualifications."

"But, you're not sure he wouldn't?" Coughlin said, prepared to grasp at straws. Leaving the Kyralean capital without a communications officer to replace Georgeo Fortuna, lost in a skirmish on Toptl, was quite out of the question. On the other hand, it was highly unlikely General Faralum would be prepared to hold up departure, considering the way political tensions had of escalating whenever General Faralum returned from the field.

"No, I'm not sure," Deil admitted. "Not one-hundred-percent sure. But, I am more sure than not sure that he won't fit in. And, I haven't come this far in my career by taking gambles that could turn against me. I'm afraid if General Faralum wants assurance that I'm giving him a suitable replacement, he must wait until I can give him more guarantees than I could ever deliver with Renson Carlylean."

"I can't believe you don't have somebody else in mind!" Coughlin said, thoroughly piqued.

"So you said," Deil said, accompanying with a nevertheless-it-is-true-that-I-don't-have-anybody-in-mind shrug.

"We transmitted our requests to you as far back as our passing of Yolani," Coughlin said.

"So you did," Deil admitted. "But, finding a replacement for you isn't exactly like finding a replacement for any other Empire spacecraft, is it? If you really want people available whenever you need them, I would suggest you bribe someone in the labovat clinic who will supply them made-to-order."

Coughlin didn't bother telling Deil that just such a project had already been initiated. However, it would still be a good many tirem before the results of that experimentation could be realized. Certainly, there would be no tangible results by the time the General's ExploraStarShips would be scheduled for departure this time around.

"Well, keep trying!" Coughlin said, getting to his feet. "If worse comes to worst, there's always the possibility that we may have to substitute one of your questionables."

"As long as General Faralum realizes I can't be held responsible."

"Of course," Coughlin said.

He didn't know why he was so upset with Deil. After all, the man had always done an excellent job. He had even been the one to pull Coughlin's name from the files and reassign him to General Faralum's staff when the vacancy arose. And, Deil was right in that the kind of men the General wanted didn't grow on trees. As a matter of fact, there seemed to be less and less of them with each new generation emerging from the crystal eggs of the labo-vats.

"In the meantime, hold off assigning the Carlylean kid elsewhere," Coughlin said. "If we have to go with a risk, it might as well be with one who's well qualified in his job category."

He exited the room, leaving a distraught Deil Magnor behind him.

Deil stretched for the Carlylean folder as soon as Coughlin was gone. He spent the next half of the morning running over it again . . . and again . . . and again.

Shortly after lunch, he sent out an order through his secretary that he wanted Renson Carlylean in his office as soon as the young man could get there.

He then attempted other work, realizing it was almost impossible to do so. Finally, he surrendered to the inevitability of it being a mostly lost day, and he plugged himself into the Relaxo-board, leaving instructions he was not to be interrupted from Dream-Sleep Sequence until Renson Carlylean made his appearance.

He was, therefore, considerably more relaxed when

Renson did arrive than he had been when Coughlin had made his earlier exit.

Lieutenant Renson Carlylean was twenty-eight. He looked younger. He was an exceptionally attractive young man with blond hair cut short in the Kyralean military tradition but which banged in a leftward sweep over his forehead. He had gray eyes with lashes and brows a good shade darker than the hair on his head, saving him from that washed-out look of many light-complexioned people. He had a pleasant nose, neither too large nor too small for his face. He had a full, somewhat pouty (though not unattractively so) mouth. His body, within the light blue uniform of his grade and rank, looked as if it had adapted well to the severe regimen of physical exercise required by any Empire officer.

"I've called you in for a bit more testing," Deil said after Renson had formally reported. "To be quite frank, there is a possibility of an assignment in the offing for which you are being considered."

Which was all he was going to say at the moment. To have admitted the position was as the communications officer on an ExploraStarShip under the command of General Faralum would have had the Lieutenant biting at the bit.

Was there a soldier in the whole military hierarchy—not knowing the facts—who wouldn't have given an arm and a leg to be assigned to duty with the great General Faralum? For Renson Carlylean, therefore, to learn that he was considered but found unqualified would have had the young man's ego damaged—possibly beyond repair. And, Deil could hardly have been able to confess that the young man's rejection had absolutely nothing to do with the official job qualifications listed in Manual 209416024.

"While I have been informed that you were scheduled for a two-week pass this evening, I'm afraid such an absence, at the moment, is quite out of the question. I would, therefore, suggest you take a few moments to make whatever calls are necessary to amend your previously made plans. You may feel free to use the tele-communicator in my secretary's office. When you have completed that, you will come immediately to Room 14-C, fifteenth level. Do you understand?"

"Yes, sir."

"Very well, then," Deil said in dismissal, watching Renson make a smart salute, execute a snappy about-face, and exit the office.

Renson Carlylean simply wasn't right. Deil could almost feel it in his bones.

Then, again, maybe he was being fooled by the young man's outward appearance of innocence. Deil reminded himself that General Jarun Faralum looked all innocence—and was anything but.

Still, Deil had a feel for these things. A feel that told him Renson Carlylean simply wouldn't fit in as an officer on any ExploraStarShip commanded by General

"Very well, then," Deil said, going to the projection cubicle and programming the timer for projection activation.

He came out and walked over to the slido-door leading into the hallway.

"Under no circumstances are you to disattach and leave the room prior to my return, do you understand?" Deil asked.

"Yes, sir."

Deil touched the light-control cube and sent the room into darkness.

He opened the door and stepped out into the hallway, sealing Lieutenant Carlylean in the room behind.

He went immediately to the adjoining room, 14-D, and opened it with his computa-key. He went up a short flight of stairs to an area that gave him visual access to the young man in the next room.

Renson, looking in the direction of where Deil was then taking a seat, would have noticed nothing but what appeared to be a solid wall. He would have heard nothing, because the soundproofing was perfect.

The timer on the projection mechanism activated the video.

A picture immediately appeared on the screen of a Dirugi warrior preparing for ceremonial self-disembowelment.

CHAPTER FOUR

The High Commander didn't want to look in the reflecto-glass, but he did anyway. It was a nightly ritual that possibly had masochistic undertones.

Or, maybe, he was simply expecting a miracle.

"Reflecto-glass on the wall, tell me who's the handsomest. . . ?"

Nothing had changed. Nothing ever changed. There was the same face and body that had been there last night. There was still more orange hair clustered around his pathetic genitalia than could be found on his almost bald head. He was so skinny, he could count his ribs.

"One . . . two . . . three . . . four. . . ."

With a sudden shudder of revulsion, he pulled his

bed-robe back around his body, fastening the elasto-bands to conceal the sight of him until the next evening. He wouldn't indulge himself in any similar masochistic rituals in the mornings. By morning, he wouldn't have gotten over the shock of what he'd seen the night before.

Why couldn't he have been born just a little handsome? Just a little. He wouldn't have necessarily needed the striking masculine good-looks of a Jarun Faralum. But, surely, he might have inherited some good point or another from one of his ancestors. He had seen the memo-pics of his grandfather, great-grandfather, back . . . back . . . back. They had none been out-of-this-world handsome, but they had had some good points. Where The High Commander had none as far as he could determine.

Oh, he had no lack of women at his beck and call. Women who told him he was handsome, told him he performed like no other men they had ever bedded. But, how many of those women would he have found in his sleep-cushion, how many of them would he have heard complimenting him on his sexual prowess, if he hadn't been who he was?

He came out of the refresh-room, immediately grouped by a squadron of his Elite Corps.

He began his nightly wander of the fortieth level of the Palace left wing. The floor held twenty royal sleep-chambers. The number had been only one before the first assassination. After that, the use of alternatives had come into being. By the time of the present High Commander's father, there had been seventeen, expanded to twenty when the recent assassination attempt had been aborted only because the intended killers had been misinformed regarding where the High Commander would be sleeping that particular evening.

Not even The High Commander knew nightly which room he would pick. If he didn't know, he figured there was little possibility of anyone else coming up with a one-hundred-percent guess.

Nightly the left wing was completely sealed off while weapons squads searched each and every sleep-chamber for intruders or for booby traps. The area stayed sealed until The High Commander retired—and then throughout the night until morning.

The High Commander almost picked the Blue Sleep-chamber, then remembered he had already slept there twice just recently. He didn't want his enemies to think he was forming any kind of a pattern. So, he picked the Emerald Sleep-chamber, although he hated green.

He stood back while two of his Corps opened the double doors. Two more members of the Corps entered with drawn weapons for yet another check of the premises. Only then did The High Commander enter, giving the room one final once-over before dismissing his men to take up positions outside the door and at every door along the hallway. The latter was a precaution lest someone be able to tell, just by looking at the door with a guard, just which chamber housed the sleeping High Commander.

Finally, the door shut behind him, The High Commander went through his own nightly routine, one born of extreme paranoia that continued even after he was alone.

He went to the sleep-cushion, arranging pillows and sheet-covers so that it appeared occupied, even though it wasn't. He then retired to one of the deep chairs off in the shadows and sat down in it, checking to be sure his weapon was handy within the pocket of his bedrobe.

He couldn't remember the last time he had enjoyed a full-night rest. Certainly it was sometime before the last assassination attempt.

The last attempt had genuinely left him with the feeling he was safe nowhere. The killers, after all, had managed to get into a sleep-chamber, despite all of the precautions to prevent them. They had been waiting for The High Commander, being ferreted behind a tapestry in a niche burrowed in the wall.

A niche for God's sake! Chiseled into solid plexistone, without anyone having heard. Or, more likely, without those who had heard doing anything about it.

The Palace was riddled with spies and traitors. He couldn't even trust his Elite Corps. He had relieved the two from duty who had killed the last attempted assassins—just because they *had* killed them and not kept them for questioning. Killing had seemed a possible method for keeping mouths shut rather than for protecting The High Commander's life.

And, now to top things off, Jarun Faralum, General Jarun Faralum, Folk Hero Jarun Faralum, arrives on the scene with his three spacecrafts stuffed to the brim with treasure. Couldn't he have once—just once—come back without being so successful? As if things hadn't been bad enough, the triumphant General Faralum had been the catalyst he always was in stirring up the dissidents who saw him as some kind of god incarnate. If those people only knew the half of it, they would know that their best bet was what they already had. But, no! They wanted a man who had flooded the kingdom with riches, who looked as they imagined a High Commander should look, whose ancestors had been royalty before The High Commander's people had come in out of the wilds, who had secrets no one would have believed.

The High Commander just might have to have Faralum killed yet. He had certainly contemplated such a course of action, held back on a couple of counts. One, he wasn't at all sure Jarun was involved in any conspiracy. Jarun's life-style, in fact, seemed to preclude his seeking the coronet of Kyrale. That, however, certainly wouldn't have prevented The High Commander, if it hadn't been for number two. Two being that the murder of Jarun Faralum would undoubtedly be blamed on The High Commander, whether it could successfully be traced back to him or not. Which was liable to be worse than having Jarun alive. There was nothing, after all, like a martyr to really get a ball rolling.

He shut his eyes. His mind drifted, coming back to reality again, drifting again. . . .

If only he could get some sleep!

There were mind-deadeners, of course. He could have even plugged into the Relaxo-board for programmed Dream Sequence. But, he would have felt trapped, locked into the euphoria, not even being able to hear his assassins sneaking up on him. At least this way, he would be able to hear. . . .

Hear? What was he hearing?

Hearing now!

His eyes came open to the darkness.

His ears strained to capture whatever it was which had brought him back to full consciousness.

Silence. That's what he heard. Only silence. Yet, there had been something within that silence, hadn't there?

There . . . *had* . . . been . . . something!

What? What?

Or was it only imagination born of paranoia?

Every muscle in his body was tense.

His eyes, now better adjusted to the dimness, searched the corners.

Yes, a sound! A faint sound, but a sound nevertheless.

Coming from where?

Caused by what?

From the door? No, not from the door.

From the window? No, not from the window.

From the ceiling! The . . . sound . . . was . . . coming . . . from . . . above.

Someone was drilling a hole over his sleep-cushion.

He sat in the darkness, too fascinated to even make an outcry. He sat and watched, trying to pinpoint the exact spot the hole would finally appear.

And, there it was! There it. . . .

The pale red of a kins-beam-ray squirted through the small aperture, drenching the sleep-cushion below to begin an immediate dissolving of it.

The High Commander aimed his lazo-gun toward the ceiling and fired.

There was a splattering of ceiling material, followed immediately by the doors swinging open to admit members of his Elite Corps.

Did they look surprised to see him? Had they expected him to be dead, part of the smoking debris that had once been his sleep-cushion?

"You stupid fools, they're upstairs!" The High Commander screamed.

His lazo-beam had blasted a hole three-feet in circumference into the ceiling plexi-stone.

More guards had followed the first into the room, now forming a thick circle around The High Commander. Some had peeled off to make a rush down the hallway to block off stairs and elevators.

Somewhere the alarm buzzer sounded, and commands were being barked.

"I want them alive!" The High Commander screamed. "Do you hear me? I want them alive!"

He then ordered an escort to take him to his office, leaving the ruined sleep-chamber behind him.

He stayed in his office, awaiting news which came shortly.

The attempted assassins had somehow managed access to the floor above the royal sleeping-chambers. Just exactly how they had gotten there, no one could rightly say. There seemed no indication of any forced entries. Which only confirmed The High Commander's suspicions that there were traitors running rife in the Palace.

Somehow (again no one seemed sure how), the attempted assassins had been signaled as to what sleep-chamber The High Commander had chosen for that evening.

They had with them a facto-drill and a kins-beam-ray machine (both found but yielding no fingerprints or other identification traces). Which pointed to even more indications of treachery within the Palace Compound. Both machines were bulky items, certainly not something one could smuggle in beneath a robe.

With the knowledge of which sleep-chamber The High Commander was using, the attempted assassins simply moved the facto-drill into place in the room above the Emerald Sleep-chamber (in this case, a deserted conference room) and had drilled away.

No one seemed to know just how the attempted assassins had seemed to know just where to place the facto-drill to produce a hole directly over the sleep-cushion in the sleep-chamber below. Then, again, an organization which had allowed the smuggling in of men and equipment, and the relaying of where The High Commander was sleeping, would have had little trouble coming up with a detailed blueprint of the Palace and the Palace furnishings, now would it?

After the hole was produced, it had been a simple matter to place the kins-beam-ray machine into place and spill a kins-beam-ray into the opening and onto the sleep-cushion below. Supposedly disintegrating The High Commander and the sleep-cushion.

Well, hadn't everyone been a bit surprised when The High Commander hadn't been in his sleep-cushion as he was supposed to have been?

The office door came open, admitting General Silas Andon, Commander of the Elite Corps. He executed a salute.

"Any word?" The High Commander asked.

"I'm afraid one was killed in a battle on the roof. . . ."

"Killed?" The High Commander screamed, coming to his feet. "I thought I told you I wanted them alive?"

"The other committed suicide before we could reach him, hurling himself over the parapet," General

Andon continued.

"And, there were only the two?" The High Commander asked, trying unsuccessfully to control his anger.

"It would seem that way," General Andon answered. "Although I have ordered extensive searches of the entire Palace Complex."

"Both dead!" The High Commander said, his face gone livid with his rage, the red clashing with the orange of his remaining hair. His fingertips were pressed so tightly against the surface of his desk that his knuckles were showing white.

"Yes, sir," the General replied. Although, The High Commander had made a statement not a question that required answering.

"The one who didn't conveniently commit suicide," The High Commander said, "was killed by whom?"

"Hard to say, Your Highness," General Andon replied. "There were ten of the Elite Corps returning fire on the roof at the time."

"Then all ten of those men are to be executed immediately!" The High Commander said loudly.

"But sir, I must. . . ."

"Don't you dare say you must protest!" The High Commander interrupted, raising his hand in a further signal for silence. "Don't . . . you . . . dare! Because, when I give an order to take prisoners alive, I mean just that. And I find it hard to believe that every assassin that enters this Palace somehow seems to be conveniently eliminated before he can be taken to interrogation."

"If you're insinuating. . . ."

"Damned right I'm insinuating!" The High Commander yelled, lowering a fist to the desk with a power that elevated papers. "I'm insinuating that there are possible members of the Elite Corps who have allegiance to other than my royal person. And, it would behoove the loyal to show their loyalty by locating the rotten apples among them and ejecting them as quickly as possible. Do I make myself understood?"

"But the executions, sir?"

"I have said all that I am going to say about the executions," The High Commander said. "And you will send me word the moment they are carried out. And if I do not have such word within the hour, you might well find yourself suspect. Do you understand that?"

"Yes, sir!" General Andon replied, giving a salute.

"Now, get out!" The High Commander commanded, waiting until General Andon was gone before collapsing back into his chair.

The tele-communicator on his desk buzzed immediately. He automatically engaged it, bringing in a video of the soldier who had taken up position in the other office.

"What is it now?" The High Commander barked.

"I have a video communication from Fila Mason," the soldier said. "It was originally routed to the left wing, coded for a wake-up. But since you were no longer in the left wing, nor asleep. . . ."

The High Commander couldn't possibly imagine what reason Fila Mason would have for trying to contact him at this time of the night, let alone have it be of such importance that she had actually requested they wake him up to receive the message.

Fila, nicknamed The Mare, looked anything like a horse. A great beauty in her time, she still retained good looks to a degree that had her occasionally still summoned to the High Commander's sleep-chamber. However, over the years, she had become less The High Commander's plaything and more the woman who watched over his total stable of girls—thus, her nickname, The Mare.

"Yes, patch Fila through," The High Commander said. If Fila was trying to reach him, it. . . .

He could tell immediately, just by looking at the way Fila looked on the videoscreen that it was something serious.

"High Commander," Fila said, "I'm afraid it's Malina."

Malina? Who in the hell was. . . .

"What about her?" The High Commander snapped. In all of the excitement, he had forgotten he had even designated Fila to send the girl to attempt spending the night with Jarun Faralum to do a little spying. Although, The High Commander had certainly not expected Jarun to take Malina up on any offers. Jarun's tastes were decidedly more exotic nowadays than a simple. . . .

"She's dead," Fila said.

"Dead?"

"Her body was just found outside the Palace walls."

"Outside? But I thought we agreed she was to be sent to General Faralum's suite this evening."

"She left for there, but the body has been positively identified as hers. They utilized her handprints for verification."

"Where is she now?"

"Morgue-room 993."

"I'll call through, then, Fila."

"I didn't know whether it was important or not, but I thought it was best to let you know anyway, considering your instructions about General Faralum and all."

"Yes, I'm glad you called," The High Commander said. "I'll get back to you later."

He asked the soldier to find the listing for Morgue-room 993 and to get them on the video. The operation took only a matter of minutes.

"Coroner Benson, Your Highness," the white-haired man identified when The High Commander came on the line.

"Yes, Coroner Benson. I'm calling about a body just picked up outside the Palace walls and identified by someone there as Malina Desina."

"Affirmative. We thought you would want to

know," Coroner Benson said, "considering she was one of your people. We did, however, go through proper channels. . . ."

"Of course . . . of course," The High Commander interrupted. "There's no question whatsoever of that. I merely was wondering if you had any indications of the murderer? I'm assuming, of course, that it was murder."

"It was murder all right," Benson affirmed. "As to whom the murderer is, we presently haven't a clue. But, I can certainly tell you one thing. Whoever it was is definitely deranged, and the sooner we get him off the streets the safer we're all going to be."

"Would it be possible to see the body?" The High Commander asked, his blood running cold.

"I'm afraid it's not a very pretty sight to see, Your Highness."

And it wasn't! The High Commander almost gagged when he saw what was left of the once attractive young woman.

After his call to Coroner Benson was completed, The High Commander took several long minutes in which to try and curb his revulsion, hoping that no one would come barging in to see his uneasy condition.

He knew what had happened to Malina, didn't he? Jarun Faralum might as well have left his fingerprints all over the body, and was, thus, trying to tell The High Commander what?

That he had somehow found out that Malina had

been sent by The High Commander and had terminated her?

If Jarun was now under the impression that The High Commander was spying on him in an effort to implicate him in a conspiracy against the crown, he might well have become more willing to accept overtures from those people responsible for the assassination attempt on The High Commander that evening.

The High Commander had to get rid of Jarun Faralum. And, since there was hardly time to arrange a satisfactory means of murder, there was only one other viable solution.

The High Commander buzzed through to the soldier out front, telling him to get Deil Magnor on the telecommunicator immediately.

CHAPTER FIVE

Renson Carlylean came awake with the lights being activated in his assigned living-cubicle. He immediately recognized the Night Captain Pierson who, upon seeing Renson come awake, had stopped midway between the open slido-door and the sleep-cushion.

"Move your butt, Carlylean!" Pierson commanded. "You've got half an hour, maybe less, to get everything—everything—packed up and ready to move out."

"I've been reassigned."

"I would say that's the logical assumption," Pierson replied.

"Where to?"

"You think they tell me shit around here?" Pierson

asked. "Hell, no! I've just been told to get you up and at it. There'll be a shuttle waiting for you by the time you're ready."

Renson quickly began gathering his things together, simultaneously wondering where he was going. So far, things were pretty irregular. Reassignments didn't usually come in the dead of night. There were usually orders ready.

He would have suspected it having to do something with the position he had been personally tested for by Deil Magnor, except that he had somehow gotten the distinct impression from Magnor that he had failed at whatever characteristics the test was supposedly out to pinpoint.

Just what the tests were supposed to prove, Renson still wasn't sure. What he had seen during the testing was some of the most gruesome and disgustingly graphic. . . .

"You ready, Carlylean?" Pierson asked, reappearing at the open slido-door.

"Will be in a second," Renson said, stuffing the last of his gear into his duffel and attaching the touch-lock.

"The shuttle just pulled up outside," Pierson said. "You'll have to sign out at the front desk, though, before leaving."

Renson shouldered his duffel and accompanied Pierson down the hallway to the esca-stairs that would take them up to the main atrium.

"You seem to be getting the VIP treatment,

Carlylean," Pierson said as the two began their ascent on the moving stairs. "The shuttle out there has Headquarter's Exec-staff markings."

"But no orders?" Renson queried, wondering if Pierson simply had made a mistake and overlooked them.

"I've been informed our copies will arrive by special courier later this evening, or sometime tomorrow morning. You'll pick up your copies at destination, wherever the hell that's going to be. Aside from that, there's little point in you trying to quiz me for information I don't have. Confidentially, I'll be just as interested to find out where you're off to as you are."

Renson signed out and walked out the door and down the steps to the waiting shuttle.

The shuttle was a fully automatic one, its computer activated when Renson's hand touched the door.

"I am programmed for delivery of Carlylean, Renson," the mechanical voice informed, just in case the wrong passenger was attempting boarding. "Would you please identify with rank and military serial number?"

"Lieutenant ZF00924A."

"Confirmed," the metallic voice said, releasing the lock. "Would you please enter, Lieutenant Carlylean? We shall begin movement in approximately five seconds."

Renson did as he was instructed, and the shuttle began movement as it had announced.

"Where exactly are we going?" Renson asked, deciding his curiosity was obviously getting the best of him.

"From here, we are to proceed by the most direct route to Exec-Headquarters," the computer replied. "There you are to be briefed by Exec-General Deil Magnor regarding your reassignment. After which, we will proceed under coordinates at the moment classified."

"But we are going to Exec-Headquarters now?"

"That is correct."

Which told Renson something was in the works if his reassignment briefing was going to be conducted personally by Deil Magnor.

Did this, then, have something to do with that series of mysterious—and strange—testing sessions Renson had been forced to endure?

He couldn't help thinking it had nothing to do with them, unless, of course, his responses had been correct ones, after all.

"What was your reaction to all of that?" Deil had asked, his voice in a practiced monotone that couldn't give hint as to which answer he was expecting, or hoping for, no hint as to which reply was right or wrong.

"I found it distasteful," Renson had answered, truthfully, knowing that the machines would have recorded his inner response no matter what he said verbally.

"Some say such things are an acquired taste," Deil

had said, unattaching the conductors from Renson's naked body.

Renson hadn't replied anything, having long ago learned that it was seldom wise, especially in test conditions, to volunteer information to anything but a direct question.

"You can get dressed now," Deil had said. He had then told Renson to come back the next morning.

The next morning had seen tests even stranger than the first day. Once again, Renson had been asked to remove all of his clothing. Only this time, he had been led into a room that resembled a dungeon from the days before the Kanberalian Wars. There he had been chained up on some seemingly medieval contraption, and while more gruesome slides were flashed on the sweaty walls, Renson was subjected to. . . .

"We are nearing Exec-Headquarters," the shuttle's computer announced, interrupting Renson's reverie. "It will be quite safe for you to leave your luggage here, as I will be taking you to your final destination when your briefing is completed."

Renson recognized the now familiar building up ahead. He had been there on and off for a two-week period, during which he had begun to wish that, whatever the position he was being considered for, he wouldn't get it. Quite frankly, he couldn't imagine any military job slot within the whole Kyralean Empire that would require the qualifications for which he had seemingly been tested.

"Exec-General Deil Magnor is waiting in Conference Room B, located to the left of the main entrance lobby," the computer informed, the shuttle coming to a complete stop by the curb. "You will be required to sign at the Night Desk, but you are expected."

The door slid open. Renson stepped out. The door slid shut and locked.

Renson walked up the stairs, pushing through the small, manually operated door that exited within the larger door that was shut and locked after office hours.

A whole array of complicated electronic equipment began an immediate surveillance, many of it weapons which—if it turned out Renson had no business being where he was—would have soon had Renson immobilized (at the least), or dead (at the worst).

The soldier at the Night Desk had a lazo-gun strapped to his right hip, although the gun remained undrawn. The soldier had, in fact, been expecting Renson (as the computer on the shuttle had indicated), and quickly gave Renson additional instructions on signing in and reaching the Conference Room wherein Deil Magnor was waiting.

"Sit down," Exec-General Magnor said, motioning Renson into one of the several chairs ringing a circular conference table.

For a moment, Renson thought that might be all Deli was going to say. The Exec-General paced while Renson sat. Magnor occasionally cast a somewhat fut-tive glance in Renson's direction. Finally, when he did sit down, it was in a chair directly across from the one in which Renson was sitting.

"You are being reassigned to the ExploraStarShip Trigon," Deil said, finally, pyramiding his hands so that his tented index fingers dimpled his lower lip.

"Trigon?" Renson asked, thinking he might have misheard.

Deil saw the expression on Renson's face, an expression he had always known would be there, probably because he had seen the same expression, time after time, registered on face after face after face.

Everyone knew the ExploraStarShip Trigon was the Command Ship under General Jarun Faralum. It had just returned with ExploraStarShips Danner-D and Kyronal-IV with holds full of the treasures from far Toptl. The ExploraStarShips Mandou-Is and Quorant had both been lost on the same expedition. Although, neither would have been lost on far Toptl if a meteorite barrage in outer space hadn't destroyed the forcefields that would have normally left the ships invulnerable to any primitive counterattacks.

"The Trigon's communications officer was killed last time out," Deil said. "The Kyralean StarShip Regulation 10/2 requires a full officer contingent on each ExploraStarShip setting out for territories beyond Strata-Rinh-12. The Trigon is presently scheduled to leave tomorrow morning on another exploration into deep space. You've been nominated to accompany."

And Deil could read the continued excitement on Renson's handsome face. Renson Carlylean . . . had . . . been . . . chosen . . . for . . . duty . . . on an ExploraStarShip under the command of THE General Jarun Faralum.

Oh, what a young fool!

"I'll be quite frank with you, Lieutenant Carlylean," Deil said. "You were not my first choice for this assignment. However, we're under pressure from time at the moment, and you got the reassignment orders because you were available."

That took a little wind out of the young man's sails.

"And I'm going to tell you why I questioned your suitability for this undertaking, because my telling you will hopefully help you to better . . . fit in."

Renson didn't say anything. What was there to say? He was so excited about the opportunity which had just opened for him, he didn't much care how the stroke of luck had come his way. If he wasn't the first choice Deil Magnor would have made, there didn't seem to be a first choice available if Deil had been forced into selecting Renson in the existing pinch.

"I have fears that you're not adaptable enough, Lieutenant Carlylean. Life aboard an ExploraStarShip, after all, is comparable to nothing for which you've presently been trained. It's a completely different kind of existence waiting for you, out there beyond the limits of . . . civilization."

Deil could have told him the connection, couldn't he? He could have told that what Renson had seen and been put through during those two weeks of testing was nothing compared to what the reality might very well become in the vacuum of deep space.

He could tell him, but he wouldn't. Why not? Because, the two most important men in the Kyralean Empire (The High Commander and General Jarun Faralum—not necessarily in that order), wanted the ExploraStarShip Trigon off the launchpad the very next morning. The High Commander and Faralum wanted the ship out of the city, each for their separate reasons. But, no matter what their reasons, what they wanted Deil wasn't about to screw up. Not since he had covered himself by telling Captain-Major Coughlin Mowler and Jarun Fowler that he couldn't guarantee the assimilability of Lieutenant Renson Carlylean. General Jarun Faralum, himself, had said Carlylean would simply have to do.

The Trigon, of course, could have violated regulation and launched without a communications officer. But, heading into deep space without a full contingent of officers wasn't quite the same as returning to civilization with a few missing, was it?

"The key to success anywhere is one's ability to bend with the tide," Deil said. "Just remember that the tides are often a bit stronger beyond the influences of civilization than you might have expected. Accepting that, and still bending, will have you hopefully doing fine."

Deil stood in dismissal.

Renson took his cue and stood, too.

"Your shuttle is waiting to take you to the ExploraStarShip Trigon in its docking area," Deil said. "You should probably go directly if you want to be securely settled into your quarters before launch time tomorrow."

CHAPTER SIX

The ExploraStarShips Trigon, Danner-D, and Kyronal-IV set a course that took them out of the Kyralean realm of influence and into deep space, passing, as they did so, through the orbits of Kimpol-IV, Disop, Coolx-2, Disnom-II, and finally approaching the planet Tibur-I. Tibur-I presently had in orbit around it a Lyro-pod from the Trigon's belly that was commanded by Sub-Commander-First-Grade Bilo Niltak.

Renson found his time occupied with a variety of jobs and functions which always proved a big difference between how one learned something in textbooks and how things were apt to be in reality.

Not that Renson in any way found himself involved

in the mysterious murkiness about which Deil Magnor had hinted. In fact, as time passed, Renson quickly forgot much of his conversation with the Exec-General, far too occupied in his new life aboard an ExploraStarShip.

An ExploraShip was somewhere in size between the streamlined BattaShips that held the perimeter of the Kyralean Empire secure from assault from within or without, and the more massive Titan Freighters which plied the spaceways of the civilized world to keep the planets sufficiently supplied with the goods and services offered by each other.

For its size and its weaponry, an ExploraShip held a comparatively small crew, probably because its missions were usually considered high-risk ventures and necessitated as little waste of qualified personnel as possible should one of them enter deep space and fail to return.

A full contingent of staff on each ExploraShip consisted of merely one-hundred men, ten of whom were officers.

Programs of on-the-job training pretty much assured that the basics of any one man's job were eventually possessed, at least to a workable degree, by one or more of the other people on board. Thus, cutting down the chances of the ship ever being completely crippled by the death of any one key crew member. Renson, therefore, often found whatever spare time he might have enjoyed from the rigors of his duties of communications officer was, more often than not, occupied with learning the intricacies of intra-ship survival systems, engine maintenance, weapons control and operation computer programming, and any other myriad job position that—if finely coordinated—kept an ExploraStarShip functioning and on the move.

Not that it was all work and no play. No rest and relaxation, Stress-Scientists had long ago discovered, brought men more quickly to the breaking point. There were several large recreation rooms for officers and for the rest of the crew, combined with a physical fitness regimen which was quickly established by the ship's physician for each and every man on board. Beyond the gym apparatus, there was a videotape projection room that ran tapes on an around-the-clock basis. There was an extensive game room and memobank library.

There was even a Pleaso-Room to which every man was allowed periodic access, since there were no females on board.

The policy of not assigning women to ExploraStarShips was not something based on a prejudicial notion that women were the weaker of the species and couldn't be expected to function adequately in stress conditions. Nor was it accountable to the fact that raiding ExploraShips were often entering into battle conditions. In a world where wars were usually far removed from prehistoric face-to-face combat, won or lost by the mere pushing of a computer button, the quick thinking capabilities of women were completely recognized as being compatible to battle situations. In fact, early ExploraShips had been staffed with both sexes, until more and more women began perishing of an illness known unofficially as The Woman Killer, and officially as *micoma-nifolicsis*, origins still unknown. While virtually nonexistent on the surface of any of the planets within the Kyralean Empire, the disease apparently struck only after prolonged exposure of artificial life-support systems to deep space, and selected only women as its victims.

The staffing of the ExploraShips with only men, therefore, had come about purely as a response to human welfare and to the fact that no ship could well afford the possible loss of several of its crew to an enemy that seemed little hindered by solid walls or forcefields. Were a cure for *micoma-nifolicsis* to be found, there was little doubt but that ExploraShip crews would once again be integrated as regarded the sexes. Until then, however, the Pleaso-Room supplied a substitute which, more often than not, was so near the real thing that it had been banned on many planets within the Kyralean Empire which still counted on natural propagation for the survival of its populations.

Renson was introduced to the Trigon's Pleaso-Room by Lieutenant Ricky Reckford, assistant to Major Fanfeld who was in charge of computer controls.

Renson easily got his bearings, since he had visited

several such installations during his university days and then during his attendance at communications school.

The process of achieving fantasy within the Pleaso-Room was easy, in that one merely stripped down and entered one of the pleaso-cylinders that could be made to automatically slip in and out of slots in the wall.

"Your request, please?" the computer voice would ask, programmed to be soft and sexy, but still managing just a touch of the mechanical that always kept it from sounding just quite perfect.

The request was then verbally relayed (acquired by a participant before entering the cylinder from a numbered letter code in index files along one wall). The mind-bend illusion then began. After which, the cylinder and its occupant were bathed in non-liquid fowlan-waves, rinsed in montolla waves, dried in non-chafing warm air, and ejected—hopefully satisfied—from the wall inserts into which the cylinder had been inserted for privacy.

What Renson soon noticed, after his first few samplings of the Pleaso-Room, was that most officers seemed to be using a separate index file in a locked cabinet along one wall. At the first opportunity, Renson asked Ricky about the cabinet.

"Oh, noticed that, did you?" Ricky said with a conspiratorial laugh. "I must say, I was wondering when your curiosity would get the best of you."

"So, what's in the locked cabinet?"

"Special fantasies," Ricky said. "Probably a bit more exotic than you're used to experiencing. Which is why they're kept under lock and key."

He laughed. He was an attractive young man. In fact, before the addition of Renson, Ricky had been the youngest officer aboard, although old enough to have accompanied General Faralum on the last expedition to far Toptl. He had brown hair, brown eyes, and a deeply cleft chin.

"No one wanted you to suddenly pick the wrong selection by mistake and get more than you had bargained for," he said.

"I'm not quite sure I know yet what you mean. How exotic?"

"That depends upon what level you decide to punch into," Ricky said. "Some of them are damned exotic, even as far as I'm concerned."

"You have a key to the cabinet, then?"

"We all do."

"All except you, then."

"Why?"

"I told you."

"They're too exotic?"

"Right."

"Says who?"

"Obviously somebody," Ricky said with a shrug. "Locking up that file index was about the first thing they did around here when they found out you were coming aboard."

"You're kidding!"

"Am I?" Ricky asked and laughed again. He had a thoroughly pleasant laugh, one that seemed to come from deep in his chest. "But, what's the problem anyway? You telling me you're not finding variety to suit you, so you want to go exploring the apparent greenness on the other side of the proverbial fence?"

"Don't be an ass! I'm merely naturally curious."

"Anyone ever tell you the one about curiosity killing the Foscat?"

"Anyone ever tell you about satisfaction bringing it back?"

"Well," Ricky said with a wide grin, "I think maybe that might depend upon the kind of satisfaction one was talking about."

"Are you for real?" Renson asked. He couldn't help but be amused by Ricky's banter. Maybe it was because Ricky had early shown an obvious inclination to form a friendship that had Renson taking such a strong liking for him now.

"Listen, Renson," Ricky said, obviously trying for a bit of seriousness. "You haven't been excluded from any key club because we've all formed some kind of a clique and decided to keep some unwanted clod out in the cold. Most of us actually like you."

"Most?"

"Well, let's face it, man, not even I am loved by everybody on board," Ricky said, his smile widening. "And, I'm certainly far more likeable than you are, aren't I?"

Renson shook his head in amused disbelief.

"If you've found a man who may be allergic to Foscats, you don't go trotting out your Foscat at the first opportunity, now, do you?" Ricky asked. "And, that, my friend, is all that's happening here."

"The locked cabinet is only for those who have Foscat fetishes?"

Ricky gave a luagh of genuine amusement.

"You want a peek at the index in that locked cabinet?" Ricky asked, as if all of this were really much ado about nothing.

"Why, you going to unlock it with your key and give me a peek?"

"Not exactly. But if you went directly to the General and told him you wanted your own key, I'd give you good odds that he'd give it to you right away. Either that, or he would simply unlock the cabinet and leave it unlocked."

"Can you see me going up to the General with a request like that?"

"Sure, why not?"

"Because I'm sure he has other more important things to occupy his time."

"You want me to ask him for you?"

"Don't you dare!"

"Just trying to be of assistance, buddy," Ricky said. "Just trying to help."

It wasn't too long thereafter, that Ricky appeared in

Renson's living-cubicle, looking like The Foscat who had swallowed the Cantiry.

"A-1-Z," he said with a theatrical flourish.

"Want to run that by me once again?" Renson asked, looking up from his desk at the man in the open doorway.

"The key to either killing the Foscat or giving him the satisfaction of clawing his way back."

"You want to give that to me in decipherable Kyralean?" Renson asked, shutting the *Manual on Repairing Possible Meteorite Damage to the Outer Protecto-Shield of an ExploraStarShip*. After the last expedition, wherein two ExploraShips had been made vulnerable by a meteorite shower (to their eventual final demise), there had been an emphasis on training as many crewmen as possible to know how to instigate patchwork repairs—if and should the need ever arise again.

"Your request, please?" Ricky said, trying his best to imitate the slightly mechanical sexiness of the computer voice in a pleaso-cylinder.

"A-1-Z?" Renson queried, thinking he might just be getting the message, but not yet sure.

"It's the very first code on the index file in the locked cabinet," Ricky said. "You're scheduled for the Pleaso-Room again soon, aren't you? Well, you tell Miss Sexy Voice to plug your mind-bend into that fantasy circuit. And, if you like the trip, you'll have carte blanche to move on from there."

"Says who?"

"General Jarun Faralum."

"You didn't ask him!" Renson said. It wasn't a question.

"He called me in this morning, and I simply couldn't pass up the opportunity," Ricky said, seeming quite pleased at Renson's obvious chagrin. "Actually, I think he'd be more than happy if you liked what A-1-Z had to offer. It would kind of clear the air that became clouded by Exec-General Deil Mangor. You know that man?"

"Yeah, he briefed me for this reassignment position."

"I guess he wasn't sure you'd . . . fit in . . . right?"

"I do recall his making some such observation."

"Well, you seem to be fitting in well enough to me," Ricky said. "General Faralum says he's had only raves so far about your performance quotient."

"He told you that—General to Lieutenant—in a friendly little chat, did he?"

"Life on an ExploraShip isn't really like life on any other known spacecraft," Ricky said, echoing what Renson could remember hearing from Deil Magnor. "After you've been on one awhile, you'll come to see it becoming less and less a case of Generals, Colonels, Majors, or Captain-Majors, and more a kind of big, happy family with fathers, uncles, cousins, and brothers. General Faralum will be having you in for a little chat, before long, too. He said it was possibly overdue already."

"Ricky, I think you're full of bullshit."

"A-1-Z," Ricky said, his wide smile showing a row of even white teeth. He turned and left Renson's living-cubicle, the slido-door whooshing shut behind him.

Every time the two met after that, prior to Renson's scheduled pass to the Pleaso-Room, Ricky would always greet Renson with a wide smile and a verbal, "A-1-Z," as if there were some possibility Renson might have forgotten since their last meeting.

On the day Renson was scheduled for the Pleaso-Room, though, Ricky was noticeably missing.

"I think he went with a party over to the Danner-D," Captain Flesiti answered when asked. "The General shuttled over for a look-see at some kind of malfunction in their tyllisic-tube structure."

Renson completed his duty and, noting his pass authorization, signed out for the Pleaso-Room.

Several people had gotten there before him, although all were already in cylinder-insert cycle, most of them (as shown by the color of the "occupied" indicator) already into mind-bend.

Renson undressed, storing his clothes in one of the banks of nearby lockers.

He ejected a vacant cylinder, crawling inside of it when its bubble lid popped up along one side. Once in, the pressure of his reclining body automatically triggered the closing of the lid and the insertion of the cylinder back into its niche within the wall.

"Your request, please?" the sexy, metallic voice asked, the sound of it seeming as if it were being purred into Renson's right ear.

With A-1-Z flashing on his brain, his lips having already formed for the beginning vowel sound, Renson didn't make the request.

Why? He wasn't sure why. Except that, maybe, something about the whole way he had come by the code index was strange and a little disturbing. What could be this fantasy and the others that they were kept under lock and key, away from him? And, why just from him?

He couldn't help remembering his two weeks of testing. Did that really have anything to do with this? Did this really have anything to do with that?"

"Your request, please?" the sexy voice repeated, having received no programmable response from the first attempt.

Yet, even as Renson continued to hesitate, he suspected he did want to fit in on this ship, didn't he? Hell, it was every man's dream to become part of the crew of an ExploraStarShip, especially under the command of the great General Jarun Faralum, Vazecry of Kahilur. And, how did Renson really fit in when there was a cabinet whose contents were only available to those having keys, Renson not having one? No matter what Ricky had said about there being no intended exclusion of Renson from any club, that was what it amounted to, in the final analysis, didn't it? And,

Renson, who had always been popular enough to be picked for all the right scholastic and social clubs throughout school, was made a little uneasy by his exclusion from this club. Although he reminded himself that the joining of any club smacked of conformity as opposed to individuality.

"The key to success anywhere is one's ability to bend with the tide," Deil Magnor had told him.

Besides, individuality really had very little place within the military structure, did it? Hadn't that been drummed into Renson from the very beginning? A fighting unit was composed of parts that had to interact together, as a group, to function properly. Individuality in war, could often gum up the works. And, any ExploraShip going into deep space was considered entering a battle zone.

"Perhaps you hgave forgotten your index code," the sexy computer voice said suddenly, having still received no instructions for fantasy interlock. "Shall I eject your cylinder to allow you a refamiliarization with the program?"

"No, that won't be necessary," Renson said.

"Your request, please?"

"A-1. . . ."

Renson was just one breath from discovering a secret, wasn't he? Just . . . one . . . small . . . breath . . . away. But, did he really want to know? Was his want to fit in suddenly counteracted by a definite fear that, knowing what was required, he wouldn't be able to comply?

"Your request, I'm afraid, is incomplete and does not compute," the female voice said, all seductive patience. "Shall I eject your cylinder to allow you a refamiliarization with the program?"

"No."

"Your request, please?"

"A-1-Z."

There was the customary pause.

There was the almost undetectable vibration.

Renson lost reality, his mind bending to the computer-induced fantasy.

A-1-Z was different from its beginning, in that Renson was thrust into a deep darkness filled with low, unsexual moans, combined with the clinking of metal against metal.

He found himself walking down a dark-cave-like corridor.

The sounds were coming from the darkness on both sides.

Up ahead, there was a pinpoint of flickering light that kept getting more and more pronounced as he approached it.

His eyes slowly began to adjust to the darkness. As they did so, he had a vague notion that he wasn't alone in the tunnel, that there were other living things along the walls, just out of his vision and reach.

He didn't stop, drawn as he was to the light up ahead as a moth was drawn to an orbit around a flame.

He stopped finally where the tunnel ruptured into a small room.

The light was supplied by several torches in brackets affixed to the walls.

Someone screamed, sending chills up and down Renson's spine.

Two men, stripped to the waist and wearing black leather hoods, appeared from the tunnel opening on the other side of the room. They dragged between them a completely naked woman with fire-red hair and a voluptuously creamy body.

Renson watched, fascinated, unable to come to the woman's aid even when the two men fastened her wrists from metal bracelets that hung from a thick chain somewhere anchored within the blackness of the ceiling above.

Both men turned toward Renson, one suddenly having a large, wicked whip in one hand.

Renson flinched automatically, thinking he was going to be beaten.

Instead, the man threw the whip to him.

"She is yours, master," the hooded man said.

Renson, horror-struck, stepped hopelessly forward, knowing full well what he was going to do.

CHAPTER SEVEN

Ricky, next time he saw Renson, didn't query about
A-1-Z, probably waiting for Renson to take the
initiative.

Renson, on the other hand, didn't mention it, because he was still too much shaken over the
experience—he felt—to discuss it rationally with
anybody.

However, the very fact that Renson didn't—when
given the opportunity—bring up the fantasy with his
friend who had arranged it, caused the relationship between the two to begin a gradual fade. Gradual, in that
it wasn't a sudden severing. Ricky and Renson, after
all, saw each other every day, often in the comparatively close quarters of the Control Deck. Nor did

Ricky quit talking to Renson in other than necessitated official capacities, even if such continued informal conversations now tended to be a little less
relaxed than they had been.

But, the relationship *did* change. Renson knew it.
Renson, also, knew why it had happened. He had
somehow failed a test in Ricky's eyes, as surely as he
had failed those other tests in Deil Magnor's eyes.
Failed, even though he didn't yet understand the purpose of the horrors endured first within the mock
dungeon of the Exec-Headquarters and, now, within
the fantasy of the pleaso-cylinder. What did any of
that possibly have to do with duty on the
ExploraStarShip Trigon?

Yet, it did have something to do with it, or why did
so many of the officers continue to select their fantasies from the file index that remained under lock and
key? Why was Ricky suddenly so distant? Why had a
prerequisite for this assignment been the two weeks of
macabre testing, conducted by Deil Magnor at Exec-
Headquarters?

Twice more, upon receiving authorization for the
Pleaso-Room, Renson did, usually bathed in sweat before and after, request A-1-Z. Each time, he emerged
as shocked as he had the first time. Probably because
the illusion was so real that it was hard to believe,
although it was the same woman each time, that his
victim really didn't die from what Renson did to her. It
was all so horribly brutal that Renson failed to see how

such a mind-bend could ever be termed a pleasurable experience.

Except that there was a continual line of officers who produced keys that unlocked even more advanced sado-masochistic fantasies. Although, Renson could shudder to think of what the more advanced fantasies consisted of if A-1-Z, the very first designate in the code file, had him whipping a woman senseless and then. . . .

He was grateful for the interruption of his reverie. It was never very enjoyable to relive his experience in the pleaso-cylinder. Even though the remembering was less intense, he found he was doing it over and over again during the day. And, at night, he was even beginning to repeat the experience in his dreams.

"I'm picking up that static again," Renson announced. It seemed a bit inconsequential, being as undecipherable as it continued to be, but General Falarum, sitting center-room in the control chair, was interested because its origins tended to arise within the unexplored region of space for which the Trigon was headed.

They were already in radio contact with Bilo Niltak around Tibur-I.

"Put it on audio for me, will you, Lieutenant?" Jarun asked.

At the same time, Jarun was carefully eyeing the young lieutenant at the communications panel. Renson was an excellent communications officer, just as Deil Magnor had predicted. But, was he material for a crew member on the ExploraStarShip Trigon? That was what Jarun wasn't yet really sure of.

Granted, Jarun had received reports that Renson had programmed for A-1-Z not once but on several different occasions. However, additional reports, mainly from Lieutenant Reckford (and, thus, to be considered reliable) indicated that Renson hadn't been willing to discuss his experiences. Which was possibly a bad sign.

Upon Renson's first reporting for duty (anyway, upon Jarun's first sighting of the young man), the Commander-General of the Trigon had hoped Renson would fit in. Renson, after all, had the highest academic qualifications, and he was an attractive young man. Scholastic record and attractiveness being two things Jarun highly prized in a member of his crew.

Jarun should, of course, have called the young man in for one of his famous Commander-crewman chats by now, except he had been hoping, especially after having found out from Lieutenant Reckford that Renson had expressed interest in sampling from the locked index file, that Lieutenant Carlylean was showing more indications of becoming one of the special breed of men who conformed to the norm of Trigon crew members.

The static from an area behind Scalic Area III went to audio, filling the Control Deck with a faint crackle that was interspersed by large and small gaps of silence. The interceptions had begun hours ago and were received at unpredictable intervals, indicating the message (if it was a message) was floating freely on a deep-space defonic warp. Which meant, it might not have originated in the area behind Scalic Area III at all.

"Can you or the computer make heads or tails out of that, Lieutenant Carlylean?" Jarun asked. "Because, it continues to sound like little more than space gibberish to me."

"Which it might very well be, sir," Renson reminded. Radio communications, distorted by tirem of travel in space, had often been known to turn up so garbled as to never be unscrambled properly.

"Yes . . . well, keep trying to make something of it, won't you?" Jarun said. "Until then, I've heard quite enough of it."

Renson rechanneled the sounds, causing them to lose the amplification of the main speakers and revert solely to those within his ear-monitor.

Following Jarun's instructions, Renson channeled the impulses one more time through the computer, with as little success as he had had the last time.

THIS DOES NOT COMPUTE! INSUFFICIENT FEED-IN! THIS DOES NOT . . .

Renson knew, of course, just why Jarun was so interested. He was interested because, except for the periodic receipt of the erratic static, there was virtually nothing emerging from that stretch of space beyond Scalic Area III.

Not only that, but there seemed to be a long stretch of virtually empty space out there somewhere in the same direction, although it was still too far away to be sure. Indications, however, did tend to indicate that there was a vacant area far larger than could normally have been expected without inclusion of some sun, planet, asteroid, comet . . . or something. Of course, that didn't mean such things wouldn't become evident as the Trigon drew closer.

The ExploraShip hadn't reached Tibur-I yet, and Scalic Area III lay a good mega-mellionic beyond that.

The static in Renson's ear-monitor came to an abrupt stop, leaving silence. It was gone but not forgotten. Renson had recorded all of it for playback through the computer whenever he thought it necessary. Hopefully, the pieces captured on tape would eventually fit together into a jigsaw out of which the computer could make some kind of comprehensive picture. That was, of course, assuming it was something more than inconsequential space noise.

Renson, then, intercepted an incoming call from the Lyro-pod Ram, in orbit around Tibur-I. A call which General Faralum, when informed of it, put through the scrambler so that Renson was neither able to hear nor record for future playback.

All of the incoming calls from Sub-Commander-First-Grade Bilo Niltak seemed to be routed through

96

the scrambler. Renson could only wonder why. Although, Renson certainly never questioned General Faralum's right to do so. Bilo Niltak had obviously been sent forward to scout out something, and his information might well have been considered of such import that General Faralum wasn't quite ready to entrust it to a communications officer whose loyalty in the field hadn't yet been tested.

The rest of Renson's duty time was relatively uneventful. Communications, as the ExploraStarShip moved deeper and deeper into space, became more and more infrequent, not only because of distances covered that necessitated lengthy delays between any messages between the Kyralean Empire and the ship, but because radio communication was often what was used by an enemy to pinpoint a spacecraft locale. And, ExploraShips, especially on missions of intended conquest, usually preferred discovery only at the last possible moment. Communication, therefore, between the Trigon and Kyralean relays had reached a point of almost virtual cutoff, except in cases of extreme emergency—which, at least, as of yet, apparently hadn't arisen on either side.

Renson took Captain Forcic, from the weapons section, through a mandatory run-through of the basics of tele-communication in deep space, part of the on-the-job-training program. He then signed out of the Control Deck area, after having turned his job over to Corporal Porscion.

As he did so, Renson couldn't help wondering if Corporal Porscion, and all of the other enlisted men, also, had a locked cabinet in their Pleaso-Room, behind which lurked an index file that would have Corporal Porscion handed a whip while a red-headed woman, her eyes filled with terror, dangled naked from chains before him.

Renson went directly to his living-cubicle and collapsed on his sleep-cushion, hands folded behind his head.

He knew Ricky was off duty, but he no longer expected Ricky to stop by. While Ricky had once always been anxious to seek out Renson's company during off-hours, that had ceased suddenly, shortly after Renson's first experience with A-1-Z.

Renson sat up on his sleep-cushion, his legs dangling over its side, his face buried in his hands.

"Some say it is an acquired taste," Deil Magnor had told him.

Was that true, though? Was it an acquired taste? No matter how many times Renson subjected himself to the sadistic trip offered him by A-1-Z, would he ever reach the point where he could enjoy it?

Why was it seemingly so important that he did enjoy it?

"I have fears that you're not adaptable enough, Lieutenant Carlylean," Deil Magnor had said. "Life aboard an ExploraStarShhip, after all, is comparable to nothing for which you've presently been trained. It's a completely different kind of existence waiting for you, out there beyond the limits of . . . civilization."

But, even if the ExploraShip was traveling in a vacuum of space populated by uncivilized worlds, wasn't the Trigon a capsule of the civilization left behind it? Simply because barbarians might suddenly inhabit the wilds outside the plexo-plasto of the ExploraShip certainly didn't require a reversion to similar barbarity within the ship, did it?

Renson simply couldn't believe that General Faralum could enter a pleaso-cylinder, program for A-1-Z (or some more advanced index code), and enjoy the experience. How could that even be a possibility?

Commander-General Jarun Faralum was the epitome of the civilized man, wasn't he? He was the undisputed envy of trillions of people within the Kyralean realm of influence. He was the role model for children and adults alike. He was educated. He was a descendant of Kyralean High Commanders. He had royal blood coursing through his veins that could be traced back to The Purple-Eyed Vazecry of Kahilur, Mumeptic Cru, who had been the first High Commander to weld together the warring planet-states into the first seeds of the present Empire.

It was inconceivable that General Faralum could enjoy the exoticism offered by that locked card index.

On the other hand, it seemed inconceivable that Lieutenant Ricky Reckford was inclined toward such exoticism, wasn't it?

But then, what kind of a man did Renson picture as being the kind drawn to the macabre turn-on to be had from dangling a woman from chains, whipping her, and then. . . .

"No, no, no," he mumbled.

It simply wasn't possible that he was expected to get into some kind of mold wherein the fantasies of A-1-Z were the rule rather than the exception.

Yet, why would Ricky steer Renson wrong? They had been friends, hadn't they? Renson refused to believe that Ricky's efforts on his behalf to put A-1-Z at Renson's disposal had been anything but admirable. Ricky had genuinely seemed anxious for Renson to fit in. He had been anxious from the very beginning. If, therefore, Renson hadn't been expected to enjoy A-1-Z, why had Ricky and everyone else suddenly seemed to pull away when it became suspected that Renson would have preferred the less exotic fare listed on the index code not locked in the cabinet?

He got up from the sleep-cushion. He went over to the computer panelboard and sat down at it.

He punched in a request to go to the Pleaso-Room. A request he expected to be denied. It hadn't been all that long since he had been there. And, while the Pleaso-Room was considered a valuable segment of ExploraShip living, it was not thought healthy for it to become a habit, anymore than any habit was considered advisable.

He was, therefore, surprised when permission was

granted, his pass-authorization number appearing on the screen.

Jotting down his number, he erased the screen, wondering why he had just done what he had done.

Did he really want to go to the Pleaso-Room? he wondered.

Some say it is an acquired taste. Was it a taste Renson was really all that anxious to acquire?

No man was an island, and Renson didn't enjoy the sudden isolation of being odd-man-out. He was a social animal. He had always gotten along with family, friends, fellow students, and associates. He had never had any trouble fitting in anywhere.

So, why was he having trouble fitting in here now?

He stood, stuffing his authorization number into the pants pocket of his uniform.

He left his living-cubicle and went to the Pleaso-Room.

Lieutenant Maxwell Deider was just preparing to enter a pleaso-cylinder when Renson signed in. Deider waved a hello. When his cylinder inserted into the wall, Renson was left alone in the room.

The "occupied" light flashed green on Deider's pleaso-cylinder, indicating a selection had been made. But what selection? Was Lieutenant Deider at that moment walking down a dark tunnel, en route to a flickering light up the way? Or was his fantasy even worse?

Renson quickly stripped and filed his clothing in a locker.

He ejected a vacant pleaso-cylinder from the wall and climbed in. The lid closed, and the cylinder quietly slipped back into the wall.

"Your request, please?" the sultry, slightly metallic voice asked in his ear.

"Your request, please?" it whispered once again a few moments later when Renson had yet to supply a programmable code.

"I seem to have forgotten my selection," Renson said. "Will you eject, please?"

"Of course," the sultry voice responded.

And, a few moments later, it was done, Renson emerging from the pleaso cylinder. He was drenched in sweat.

He was glad no one was there to see him, question what in the hell was wrong.

Something was definitely wrong, wasn't it?

He quickly washed off in one of the showers supplied for those who wished to take a more leisurely cleanse than was offered by the fowlan waves, montolla waves, and non-chafing warm air of the cylinder.

While drying, he noticed that Lieutenant Deider's light had flashed orange, indicating he was well into the initial phases of mind-bend.

Renson dressed, left the Pleaso-Room, but didn't head back for his living-cubicle but for Commander-General Faralum's suite of rooms on the twelfth level, detouring for Major Zammer's quarters only when he realized that a Lieutenant didn't go barging in on a General but had to go through a chain of command. He figured himself in bad enough shape without attempting to alienate his superiors by going over their heads.

Major Zammer seemed exceedingly understanding, especially since it was obvious Renson had interrupted him in the middle of his meal. He hardly seemed even surprised by Renson's request to see the General, although he did go through all the standard motions to head Renson off.

"You're sure this is nothing I can help you with, Lieutenant?" Major Zammer asked. He was a handsome man, probably somewhere around sixty tirem. His startlingly white hair (acquired at birth and not the result of aging) was attractively banged over deep, friendly blue eyes.

"I'm afraid not, sir. As I said, it's somewhat of a delicate, personal nature."

"And it's not something you feel you can settle for yourself?"

"No, sir, I don't believe it is."

"Why don't you let me see what I can do to arrange something then?" Major Zammer said with a fatherly smile. "You go back to your living-cubicle, and I'll get back to you as quickly as possible. All right?"

"Yes, sir," Renson said, giving a smart about-face and heading for the slido-door.

"And, Lieutenant Carlylean?" Major Zammer said just before Renson reached the door.

"Yes, sir," Renson said, turning back from the door and toward the Major who was still seated at his table.

"I can't tell you how anxious we all are, my boy, for you to get over whatever it is that's bothering you. You are a skillful communications officer and a thoroughly likable young man."

"Thank you, sir," Renson said. More than a little surprised by the compliment.

"I'm sure if we just take everything one step at a time, it will all work out well in the end, don't you?"

"I hope so, sir."

"We're all so very anxious for you to fit into our little family."

"Thank you, sir."

"Now, I'll see what I can do about getting you in to see General Faralum," Major Zammer said, getting to his feet.

Renson couldn't have been back in his living-cubicle more than a few minutes before Major Zammer punched through on the viewer screen.

"The General is waiting for you in his suite of rooms on the twelfth level, my boy," Major Zammer said. "You do know where it is?"

"Yes sir."

"He's looking forward to seeing you," Major Zammer said. "He's been planning on getting together with you for quite some time now. You being a new man on board, you know? New men often have minor adjustment problems—in the beginning."

"Yes sir."

"Well, I won't hold you up any longer, my boy," Major Zammer said. "As I mentioned, the General is waiting for you now, and it wouldn't be proper or good policy to keep him waiting, would it?"

"No sir."

"Just tell the man on the outer desk that you're expected. I'm sure you'll have no problems."

"Thank you, sir."

"Don't mention it, Lieutenant. And don't hesitate to come to me if anything else is ever bothering you."

Major Zammer punched out.

By the time the ele-tube was signaling the approach of level twelve, Renson was beginning to wonder if he hadn't made some kind of very big mistake.

Just what was he going to say when he was finally ushered into the presence of General Faralum? Was he actually prepared to demand an explanation as to what in the hell was going on? Did he actually expect the General to come right on out and tell him why everyone seemed so anxious that Renson not only experience the horrors of A-1-Z but enjoy them?

The Sergeant on the outer desk, present the moment the ele-tube door slid upward to exit Renson on the twelfth level, not only knew Renson (with only ten officers on board, it was hard not to know all of them), but had been expecting him.

"Pin this to your right breast pocket," the Sergeant said, handing Renson a plasto-clip with his name and picture engraved on it. "And have it ready to show the Corporal at the end of the corridor. The Corporal, in turn, will show you where to go from there."

The Corporal directed him down another corridor to a Sergeant-Major. The Sergeant-Major directed Renson into the General's suite.

General Faralum was waiting. Not behind a desk as Renson had been expecting. Not in his official uniform, either.

He was attired in an informal night-robe that had Renson immediately suspecting his appointment had interrupted the General's plans to retire.

"Yes, Lieutenant Carlylean, isn't it?" Jarun said.

Rather than return the young man's salute, Jarun came forward to offer his hand. After the shake, he motioned Renson over to one of the comfor-cushions that were scattered around the room. He then turned to the Sergeant-Major who hadn't yet left.

"Pour the Lieutenant and me a drink of ambrosina, will you, Sergeant-Major?" Jarun asked, taking a cushion across from Renson. He gave the young man an obvious appraisal while waiting for the requested drinks to arrive.

The mildly alcoholic ambrosina was in a servo-cabinet off to one side. It only took the Sergeant-Major a few seconds to obtain the drinks and serve them. After which Jarun dismissed him.

"Now," Jarun said, sipping from his vee-shaped crystal, "Major Zammer informs me that you're having some kind of personal problem."

Renson was somewhat disconcerted by the surrounding informality. There was something disturbing about the way the General's eyes were focused on him, too.

"There *was* some personal problem, wasn't there?" Jarun asked, as if there was the possibility he might have been mistaken.

"Yes," Renson admitted, taking a swallow of ambrosina in a hopeful attempt to lubricate his suddenly bone-dry throat.

Jarun waited patiently, his curious purple eyes not leaving Renson for a minute.

Renson realized he was beginning to sweat. He could feel virtual rivers of perspiration forming in his armpits and drooling down his sides. He took a deep breath, deciding that—having come this far—it would have been ridiculous to pretend having made a mistake in coming.

"Personal problems, once out in the open, are usually not half as insurmountable as they sometimes seem when kept inside of us," Jarun said by way of encouragement. "In fact, I rather approve of my men admitting to certain problems, seeking to find solutions, rather than filing them away in some attempt to pretend they don't even exist."

"There is a locked cabinet in the Officers' Pleaso-

Room," Renson said, embarrassed to hear his voice coming out somewhat like a croak. "I was once told that the quickest way of getting a key was by coming to you and asking for one."

"Here," Jarun said, reaching into the pocket of his night-robe, "use my key, please."

He produced the key and tossed it across the floor to where Renson could reach it.

"And when you unlock the cabinet, you might as well leave it that way from now on," Jarun said. "Then there'll be little need of any of us to have keys, right?"

The way the key had conveniently been in Jarun's pocket had Renson immediately wondering if the General had anticipated the reason behind Renson's visit.

"See how easily previous problems are solved if brought out into the open?" Jarun said, his appraisal of Renson having decided it would be a genuine pity for all involved if the young man didn't work out. "Actually, I would have seen you had a key from the very beginning if I had suspected you of really wanting one. I don't know why, but I was somehow led to believe that A-1-Z really wasn't to your liking."

Renson had been in enough test situations in his life to know that he was in one right then. And he still wasn't exactly sure how he should respond. Except that there had been unmistakable clues, all along the way, hadn't there?

"A-1-Z was something a little new for me," Renson

said. "It's taken me a little time to try and decide just how I do react to it."

"And what have you decided?" Jarun asked, casually sipping more ambrosina, as if he had just asked the most innocuous question possible.

Except that Renson recognized the loaded question when he heard it.

"I've decided I need a little more in-depth research before deciding definitely," Renson said finally.

"Which you hope to find in the locked cabinet?"

"Yes, sir."

Jarun settled back in his comfor-cushion, eyeing the young blond over the lip of his vee-crystal.

"You are an exceptionally intelligent young man," Jarun said after a short pause. "I've seen that spelled out in the figures recorded in your file. I've seen that by watching the way you perform your duties, and by getting reports from men I have come to trust. I see it now by talking to you face-to-face. Intelligence is a commodity I value highly. If things work out, there is nothing I would rather do than welcome you aboard the Trigon as a permanent member of my crew. On the other hand, if things don't work out, I'm sure you're intelligent enough to realize it will have had nothing whatsoever to do with your abilities to carry out the duties of a communications officer. And there are other ExploraShips besides those under my command; there are other spacecraft whose captains would more than be pleased to welcome you aboard—if things don't work out for you here."

And Renson realized that the General couldn't have made it any more clear than that, could he? The only means to total acceptance on the ExploraStarShip Trigon did, indeed, have something to do with the index file in the locked cabinet.

"You do all the in-depth research you wish to do in order to make a decision, Lieutenant," Jarun said. "Do so with my blessing. And if you come to decide, in the end, that you're not really suited to the world we would all like very much to have you become a part of, you need only remember that this expedition will not last forever. Eventually we will return to Kyrale, and with my recommendation behind you, you'll be welcome most anywhere. So. . . ."

He came to his feet, placing his glass on a tri-table off to one side.

Renson took his cue, coming up, too, his glass in one hand, the General's key to the locked cabinet in the other. He placed the glass on the tri-table in order to once again experience the firm grip of the General's hand. His other hand had gone clammy around the key.

"I'll be most happy if you would report to me regularly on your progress," Jarun said, his arm around the younger man's shoulder as they walked toward the slido-door. "There are several of us, Lieutenant Reckford in particular, who will be most anxious to wish you well."

"Yes, I shall be sure to keep you posted," Renson said, his voice sounding strange ... strange ... strange.

"And you'll be returning now to the Pleaso-Room?" Jarun asked, pausing at the door and flashing Renson a friendly smile.

Of course he knew. There was probably very little on the ship he didn't know, including the fact that Renson had requested a pass for the Pleaso-Room, had gone there, but failed to enter mind-bend.

"What intelligent person wouldn't utilize a pass to the Pleaso-Room?" Renson said, smiling nervously.

"Then I shall wish us all luck, Lieutenant Carlylean," Jarun said, activating the slido-door.

The Sergeant-Major was waiting on the other side to show Renson the way out.

Renson went immediately back to the Pleaso-Room.

At first he thought the key wouldn't fit the lock, then realized it was his own nervousness which was making the difficulty. Turning the key over, consciously willing his hand to keep from trembling, he fitted the key perfectly. And when he turned the key, the lock disengaged.

He deposited the key in his pocket and opened the cabinet to reveal the index-file.

At the very front was card A-1-Z, giving a synopsis of the fantasy Renson had already experienced several times in the cylinder.

He flipped to A-1-Y, read the synopsis and shivered.

By the time he had read A-1-G, he suspected he was losing his nerve. How could he be expected to live through such fantasies, let alone enjoy them?

Yet his enjoyment was a prerequisite for his becoming a permanent member of the crew, wasn't it? And although he might very well have found a position on some other ExploraShip, or on some other Kyralean spacecraft, it was assignment to one of Jaran Faralum's ships which was considered the most plum position, wasn't it? Anything after this would be paramount to an demotion, at least in the eyes of Renson's peers.

Renson had always striven for the highest pinnacles. Up until now, he had reached his objectives with very little trouble. Was he going to surrender now, just because this plum wasn't as easily picked as all the others had been?

"Some say it is an acquired taste," Deil Magnor had said.

An acquired taste . . . an acquired taste . . . an acquired taste.

He flipped to card A-1-M, purposely not reading the synopsis. He closed the index, but not the cabinet. The General had told him to leave the cabinet unlocked, since there was no longer any need for keys.

He went to a locker and undressed. He deposited his clothes, pausing to use his T-shirt to wipe the latest glaze of sweat from his face, chest and belly.

A-1-M.

He walked over to the wall of pleaso-cylinders, ejecting a vacant one from the wall at the same moment Lieutenant Maxwell Deider was ejecting at the completion of his cycle.

Maxwell, who had seen Renson preparing for mindbend when he had first entered his pleaso-cylinder, was somewhat surprised now to see Renson preparing to enter one.

"You surely aren't out for repeats!" Maxwell said in obvious amazement.

There were men who could take consecutive mindbends, but Maxwell had never met one.

Neither had Renson.

"No," Renson replied with a laugh. "I decided to go see the General first and pick up my key."

He nodded toward the cabinet he had left open.

"The General said there's little point in continuing to leave the cabinet locked now that we all have keys," Renson added.

"Damn, that's great news!" Maxwell said, seeming genuinely pleased. "What mind-bend are you taking?"

"A-1-M," Renson said, wishing suddenly he had picked something so advanced it would have really impressed Maxwell.

Maxwell, though, already seemed impressed.

"I actually prefer the A-Series," Maxwell said. "A-1-M, now, is one hell of a good mind-bend. Rimsky, now . . . you know Rimsky?"

Renson knew him, but not well.

"The Captain in Maintenance, isn't he?"

"Yeah. Well, he's into the X-Series, if you can believe that. I tried an E once and wondered if I'd ever make it back."

"I'll remember that," Renson said, wondering why Maxwell was so talkative. While Maxwell had never been unfriendly before, he had certainly never gone much beyond nodding a hello.

"Listen, when you're through here, why don't you come on down to my cubicle and shoot the bull?" Maxwell said, surprising Renson even more. "I'm having a few of the guys in, but you know most of them. Ricky Reckford will be there. He was saying just the other day how he missed not seeing more of you."

"Yea, maybe I will stop by," Renson said. "That is if Zammer doesn't have something in the works. He was talking special duty later this evening."

Renson wanted an out, just in case A-1-M ended up leaving him as drained as A-1-Z had. If that were the case, he would have been defeating his purpose by showing up looking as if he venture into acceptable mind-bend had left him nauseously drained.

"Well, drop by if you can," Maxwell insisted.

"What mind-bend did you go through just now?" Renson asked, suddenly curious.

"A-2-F," Maxwell said. "You might keep it in mind. It's one hell of a turn-on."

"Yea, maybe I will," Renson said, mentally noting that Maxwell had emerged from the mind-bend looking as if he had just had eight good hours of sleep.

"Well, don't let me keep you any longer," Maxwell said. "And congratulations again on getting that damned cabinet unlocked. It was a pain in the ass when locked permanently."

Renson climbed into the pleaso-cylinder, watched the lid drop, felt the slide of his cylinder into the wall.

"Your request, please," the sultry computer voice asked.

"A-1-..."

He stopped, remembering again how refreshed Maxwell had appeared.

"Correction, please," Renson said.

"Correction noted," the sultry voice replied.

"A-2-F."

"Correction to A-2-F, is that correct?"

"Yes."

There was the customary pause.

There was the almost undetectable vibration.

Renson lost reality, his mind bending to the computer-induced fantasy.

He found himself in a room full of naked men, women, and children.

He was dressed. In black boots. In black riding pants. In black military blouse with lightning-bolt insignias on his collar.

For a moment, he thought he was the only one dressed, until he noticed more similarly dressed men, positioned elsewhere around the room.

His eyes wandered elsewhere, up and down the lines of naked people.

He pushed his way through the crowd, striking out indiscriminately with the riding crop he held in his right hand, hitting at anyone who even seemed to be preparing to get in his way.

He stopped finally. He reached out his left hand, clamping his thumb and fingers upward around the chin of one of the prisoners.

These . . . naked . . . people . . . were . . . all . . . prisoners!

He turned the face toward him.

It was the face of a young boy. A very scared young boy whose naked body Renson proceeded to survey as if he were looking over meat in a butcher shop.

"Come with me, scum!" Renson commanded loudly.

CHAPTER EIGHT

"Some say it's an acquired taste," Deil Magnor had told him.

And maybe it was an acquired taste.

Anyway, Renson was beginning to think that—until what happened in orbit around Tibur-I. Then it all changed.

It was one thing to indulge in sado-masochistic fantasy in the pleaso-cylinders. That being pure fantasy—albeit real enough to pass for momentary reality. But one could adjust to that, remembering that there was nothing more exciting than a good horror film. And the experiences in the pleaso-cylinders were nothing more than horror films played out in the brain. Horror films in which one seemingly became a participant in the action. Anyway, that had become Renson's rationalization, made easier when he came to discover how a successful rationalization allowed him suddenly to fit in, where he hadn't really fit in before.

Suddenly he had become one of the group, someone no longer on the outside looking in. Ricky came back, taking up their friendship right where it had left off, as if nothing whatsoever had happened in the interim. Others like Maxwell Deider, officers who had previously said very little to Renson, seemed to compete for his favor. There were all-night gab sessions, card games, general all-around blowing off steam, all in which Renson was now included.

Even his superiors seemed pleased with his progress. Major Zammer informed him, just prior to rendezvous with the Lyro-pod Ram off Tibur-I, that Renson had just been nominated for an upgrade to Lieutenant-Captain.

"We're very pleased with the way you've managed to fit in, my boy," Major Zammer had said. "I'll not deny that you had some of us extremely worried there for a while."

And if his regularly occurring sessions in the pleaso-cylinder still tended to leave him a little nauseous, he told himself that no one else exposed to the same ordeals seemed to look any the worst for wear.

All things aside, Renson had decided his bargain, even if possibly struck with the Devil, had come out advantageously to his side.

Then came Tibur-I.

Renson had, of course, been well aware of the air of excitement prevailing on board the Trigon in those space-days prior to the rendezvous. As the Lyro-pod Ram came nearer and nearer, now actually a spot recognizable on the space-scanner viewer screen, the excitement built accordingly.

"What's this Sub-Commander-First-Grade Niltak like?" Renson had finally asked, sequestered at the time with Ricky, Maxwell, and Lieutenant Lxic in Lxic's living-cubicle.

"A Z-Series," Lxic had replied immediately.

Renson had soon learned that most everyone was categorized by the level of fantasy in which he most frequently indulged. Renson and Maxwell were A's, Lxic and Ricky were B's.

"I know that's the rumor," Maxwell had said. "But do you really believe it?"

"I have to believe it," Lxic said. "The computer tapes don't lie. And I saw the computer tapes."

The computer tapes were the written readouts that recorded on plasto-paper each day what was verbally put into the computer. As requests to the pleaso-cylinder were verbal, those were daily recorded.

"Swear to God?" Maxwell pressed, still obviously a little dubious.

"Which one?" Lxic asked with a smile. He was an agnostic.

"Which one is in vogue at the moment?" Maxwell asked. He didn't much believe in Supreme Beings either, unless there was a Big Computer somewhere in the sky.

"Well, there seemed to be a revival of the teachings of The Teacher Chyrosto in Kyrale this last time in," Lxic said. "Do you think he'll do?"

"Sure, why not?" Maxwell conceded.

"Then I swear by the sacred vital organs of Chyrosto, as they were shed by the Wyolean meat-cleavers on Folon-Vilic."

"Mmmmm," Maxwell hummed, still seemingly unconvinced.

"Why would I lie?" Lxic asked. "It's no skin off my balls if he's an A or a Z."

"He just doesn't remind me of a Z-Series," Maxwell said in admission.

"You mean General Faralum does?"

"General Faralum is a Z?" Renson asked, a little surprised to hear that. Although, simultaneously, he wasn't sure just why he was surprised.

"I hear he's more than a Z," Maxwell admitted. "Although I can't begin to fantasize where in the hell that mind-bend would take him."

"He doesn't look like he would be a Z, now does he?" Lxic observed triumphantly. "Well, the same holds true for Niltak."

"What's Niltak look like?" Renson queried, remembering it was comments on Niltak which had brought the conversation in this direction in the first place.

"He looks like the kind of big brother anyone would love to have," Maxwell said.

"A kobasal-bear quality," Lxic said. "Kind of cuddly."

"Cuddly?" Maxwell asked, laughing incredulously.

"That's how my mother described him," Lxic said, looking a little embarrassed.

"Anyway," Maxwell said, "He's really a good guy. And he's a damned good fouson ballplayer. We'll have to line up some games after we get into deep space and away from all this shakedown routine."

"Anyone know what he's doing in orbit around Tibur-I?" Renson asked, that being a subject that had had him curious for a long time.

General Faralum's communications with Niltak had continued going through the computer scrambler.

"Interrogating the natives, I should imagine," Lxic said with a wide grin.

"If there are any natives left by the time we get there," Maxwell said.

He and Lxic laughed at what apparently as an insource of amusement. Realizing suddenly that Renson really hadn't been around long enough to catch the humor, they came back to the conversation at hand.

"We're looking for the Cities of Zythin, right?" Maxwell asked Renson.

"Right."

"Well, there have been hints of the Zythineans having touched down on several planets in their trek across space. A planet called Kimpol-IV, another called Disop, another called Coolx-2, and one called Disnom-II. If you sit down at an astro-chart and connect those planets with a line, taking into account certain long-existent rumors that the Zythineans eventually settled somewhere beyond the Scalic Area III, you come up with conjecture that they might have stopped off at several other planets too."

"One of which might have been Tibur-I?"

"Right!" Lxic answered.

"So Niltak was sent to Tibur-I in the search for possible clues linking to a Zythinean touchdown?" Renson asked.

"That's the way we've all got it figured," Lxic affirmed.

"Wouldn't he have about as much chance of success as finding a pseedle in a pile of kyrofoam splinters?" Renson asked.

"Niltak, I assure you, can be most persuasive with the primitives," Maxwell said. "If there's any folk legend on Tibur-I about furry pinwheels from outerspace, you can bet your ass that Niltak will have found it."

Renson's first official look at Sub-Commander-First-Grade Bilo Niltak came after the docking of the Trigon with the Lyro-pod Ram. General Faralum hosted festivities for the officers of all three ExploraStarShips under his command, ferrying the officers from the Danner-D and the Kyronal-IV to the Trigon via space shuttle.

Bilo was younger than Renson had expected. As both Maxwell and Lxic had commented, he didn't look anything as Renson would have imagined someone deeply into the Z-Series of mind-bends.

He appeared to be somewhere around forty tirem; but, his grade and rank would seem to have indicated he was a lot older. It simply didn't happen that anyone—no matter how good he was, or whatever his connections—ever made it to sub-commander-first-grade status at forty. Still, he did look that young.

He had brown hair and golden eyes, the latter hinting of a possible Keanterbind in the woodpile.

He had pleasant features. Not strikingly handsome, with a too-perfect look that made him look unreal, but with the kind of good looks had by an attractive man-next-door type.

When he laughed (and he laughed quite often, even before the ambrosina started flowing), the sounds were infectuous, spreading to everyone within hearing around him.

He seemed to enjoy physical contact, usually placing his right hand on anyone's shoulder who seemed to be talking to him at the moment.

He and General Faralum seemed to be the best of friends. Even though they maintained the correct decorum of sub-commander-first-grade toward commander-general, it was easy to see, by the way they related to one another, even under formal conditions, that they were probably a good deal more intimate in private.

"Ah!" Bilo had exclaimed upon receiving introduction to Renson in the receiving line. His golden eyes seemed to take Renson in—not uncomplimentary—at a glance. "So, this is the Lieutenant Carlylean I've been hearing so much about."

"That depends upon what you've been hearing," Renson said, almost immediately being drawn to the man.

Bilo didn't release his firm grip of Renson's hand, but added his left hand to additional cup it.

"All good things, I assure you," Bilo said. "I shall certainly be looking forward to seeing more of you. Maybe we can even arrange for you to sit in on a little interrogation I have lined up in the Lyro-pod before we blast free of the orbit." He turned to General Faralum who was in the receiving line next to him. "What do you say, General? Is Lieutenant Carlylean here on the invitation list?"

"I haven't quite decided yet," Jarun answered truthfully, turning to Renson. "How are you, Lieutenant Carlylean?"

"Fine, thank you, sir."

"We'll all three get together and talk about it later, right? Your attendance at the interrogation, I mean."

"Yes, sir," Renson replied, recognizing just a trace of reticence—if not seemingly hostile—for Bilo's

124

suggestion, at least as far as the General was concerned.

"I'll put in a good word for you, Lieutenant," Bilo said with a friendly wink.

Bilo, then, albeit reluctantly, released Renson's hand and greeted the next man in the line.

"And my, but didn't it look as if you were getting chummy with Sub-Commander Niltak," Lxic said, coming up to Renson in the crowd a little later. "We thought he was going to never turn loose of your hand and give the rest of us a go. What in the hell did you two have to talk about?"

Before Renson could answer, however, Ricky had joined them, just as anxious as Lxic to find out what had gone on between Renson and Bilo in the receiving line.

"Nothing but small talk," Renson assured.

"Lieutenant-Captain Sleser said he overheard a mention of an interrogation," Ricky said.

Lieutenant-Captain Sleser, an officer from the Danner-D, was the man who had gone through the line immediately ahead of Renson.

"No shit?" Lxic asked, obviously impressed.

"Well?" Ricky pressed Renson. "Did he say something about an interrogation?"

"What's coming off here?" Renson asked curiously. He could more than tell that both Ricky and Lxic were obviously excited. "No matter what he said, I assure you it was only something to make conversation. I'm not too sure I even remember what he said, to tell you the truth."

"Well, rack that memory of yours, you lucky bastard," Ricky said. "Did he say anything about an interrogation?"

"Why don't you tell me what's suddenly gotten into you two?" Renson said. "You look as if you've got pic-ants in your pants."

"About that mention of an interrogation?" Maxwell said, joining the threesome.

"So, maybe he did mention something about one," Renson admitted.

"*Maybe* he did?" Maxwell said excitedly. "Either he did or he didn't, my boy."

"Something about his having one lined up in the Lyro-pod before breaking orbit around Tibur-I, wondering if I'd be interested in attending."

"Sweet Mother of Chyrosto!" Maxwell said, his voice dipping to a mere whisper. "You lucky sonofabitch!"

"Getting invited to an interrogation is supposed to be some kind of big deal?" Renson asked, a little un-sure why a question-and-answer period (obviously to be directed at some Tiburian primitive) should have any reasonable aspects to excite his friends.

"Well, let's put it this way," Ricky said. "If you do get an invitation, and you don't decide to go, keep your old buddy here in mind to stand in for you, won't you?"

"Why in the hell should he remember you?" Lxic asked.

"When he's got me standing by to take on his overloaded social schedule," Maxwell added.

"It was nothing but small talk," Renson assured. "In fact, General Faralum didn't seem any too taken by the proposal."

"General Faralum?" Ricky asked. "What did he have to say about any of this?"

"Come on, you guys," Renson said. His vee-crystal was empty of ambrosina, and he was looking for a refill. "Let's drop this, huh? It's just too ridiculous to make such a big thing out of a couple of seconds of hurried conversation in a receiving line."

"Why don't you tell us how General Faralum happened to get his two-credits worth into this?" Lxic said, indicating that he, for one, had no intentions of letting the conversation drift elsewhere.

Renson was persuaded more by the fact that he managed to retrieve a full vee-crystal of ambrosina from a passing tray, without moving, than by anything else.

"Sub-Commander Niltak asked General Faralum if I had been put on the invitation list," Renson said.

"So, do you believe it? Do you . . . believe it?" Lxic said, turning to Ricky and Maxwell.

"Niltak really asked the General that?" Ricky wanted to know. "Right there in line? You are living under the right stars!"

"Before you get carried away, from whatever unknown reasons, I'll have to confess that General

Faralum seemed little enthused by the notion of my presence."

"Like, what did he say?" Maxwell asked.

"*Exactly* what did he say," Ricky chimed in.

" 'I haven't quite decided yet. How are you, Lieutenant Carlylean?' To which I replied, 'Fine, thank you, sir! To which he replied, 'We'll all three get together and talk about it later. . . .' "

"Lieutenant Carlylean?" someone asked, it being neither Maxwell, Lxic nor Ricky, but the Corporal who had been passing around the tray of vee-crystals. Since Renson didn't recognize him, he assumed the Corporal had been brought over for the occasion from one of the other two ExploraShips.

"I'm Lieutenant Carlylean," Renson said.

"I beg your pardon, sir. But Commander-General Faralum wondered if he might have a moment of your time?" He nodded toward the spot where the General and Bilo Niltak were talking together.

Bilo caught Renson's glance in his direction and waved.

"If you will excuse me, then?" Renson said, bowing to his companions before leaving them.

"And if you forget any word that's said during the next few minutes, your friends shall boil you in oil!" Ricky whispered after him.

Renson began his weave through the crowd. On several occasions, people tried to stop him, attempting to bring him into their conversation. In each instance, they immediately released him upon learning by whom he had been summoned.

"Lieutenant Carlylean!" Bilo exclaimed, his voice having a way of registering genuine delight, as if it had been a tirem since the two of them had last seen each other, rather than just a few minutes. "I have some good news for you and some bad. First, the good news. General Faralum has consented to let you attend the little interrogation I've scheduled for later this evening. The bad news being the General insists you take a silax-capsule before going."

"A silax-capsule?" Renson asked. He wasn't familiar with the drug.

"A product of the primitives on Sim," Bilo explained. "Which is probably why you never heard about it before. As a matter of fact, the General and I are the only two people I know who have a supply."

"I'm afraid I'm a little confused," Renson admitted.

Before he could receive any immediate elucidation, however, they were joined by the Sergeant-Major whom Renson recalled from his visit to the General's suite of rooms.

"You asked for this, General?" the Sergeant-Major said, extending a gold-green capsule between his thumb and forefinger, which Jarun immediately removed.

"Yes, thank you, Sergeant-Major," Jarun said in dismissal. He turned and handed the silax-capsule over to Renson.

Renson could do little more than look at it, wondering what exactly a silax-capsule was supposed to do, considering it was a condition the General had made to his attending an interrogation.

"It's quite harmless, I assure you," Bilo said, flashing one of his friendliest smiles. "And such a small price to pay, don't you agree?"

"As I've told you, Bilo," General Faralum said, "I do believe the Lieutenant hasn't the faintest notion as to what your interrogations are."

"Then he is in for a treat, isn't he?" Bilo said with a laugh. He turned his warm, golden eyes on Renson. The eyes had dark centers. "Come on, Lieutenant, trust me."

So what was Renson going to do? Say no? Say he wasn't the kind to put strange chemicals into his system without first knowing what they could be expected to do to him? Tell the General and the Sub-Commander that he could care less about an interrogation?

He put the capsule on his tongue and swallowed it with a quick gulp of ambrosina.

"Excellent!" Bilo exclaimed.

Even General Faralum looked pleased.

"We won't be leaving for a while yet, Lieutenant," Jarun informed. "If you would like to return to your friends, I'll see that you're summoned at our time of departure."

"Yes sir. Thank you, sir."

130

Maxwell and Lxic got to him before anyone else could. It was Renson though who got in the first question.

"What in the hell is a silax-capsule?"

"A what?" Maxwell and Lxic responded in perfect unison.

"A silax-capsule. Green and gold."

Maxwell shrugged. Lxic mimicked his movement.

"Beats me," Maxwell said. "What's that got to do with the price of filoon in Caslook?"

"You trying to divert our attention from the real issue at hand?" Lxic asked. "Or, have you been instructed to keep secrets by your superiors in command?"

"Actually, it looks as if I'm going to an interrogation later this evening," Renson said, suddenly wanting to gloat a little in front of his friends. The truth being, the only reason he was even vaguely enthused was because his friends seemed so damned envious.

"Would you believe an A is being invited to an interrogation being conducted by a Z?" Lxic asked, as if some people got all the breaks.

"Who knows, maybe the General is doing the honors?" Maxwell suggested.

"And wouldn't that be wild for Lieutenant Carlylean!" Lxic exclaimed.

Renson, meanwhile, was feeling strange things happening inside of him. Although he would have been hard-pressed to exactly put his finger on them. In fact, neither Maxwell nor Lxic noticed any outward difference at all.

"Just wait until this gets around?" Maxwell announced. "As a matter of fact, I can't wait to be the one to start the juicy gossip on its way."

"Maxwell, please try to keep a button on your lip, will you?" Renson said. "I know the General didn't tell me to keep my mouth shut, but just maybe he was assuming I would use a little discretion."

"No one has ever kept an interrogation secret yet for as long as I've been on board," Lxic observed.

"So, what's the good news?" Ricky asked, joining the party. "I got cornered by that Miller, and thought to hell I was never going to be able to break free."

"Would you believe Renson here has just been invited to an interrogation?" Maxwell asked. "This very night."

Renson groaned.

It didn't take long for the word to spread, and it soon became apparent that Renson's friends weren't the only ones who were talking. Before Renson was asked if he would, once again, be kind enough to join the General, he had been informed by Maxwell, Ricky and Lxic as to just whom the other members of the lucky party were going to be. A list which, considering the way it was acquired, turned out—as Renson was later to discover—to be pretty much accurate.

In fact, as the only one below Major on the invitation list, Renson was keeping decidedly illustrious company. Or, so informed Maxwell before telling Renson to be sure and remember his friends when he came back down to ground zero.

The selected group was transported to the Lyro-pod Ram in intra-ship shuttles. As the pod was docked with the Trigon, there was no inconvenient necessity to shuttle through space.

The intra-ExploraShip shuttles were comparatively small, and Renson found himself riding alone in the last one with Bilo.

"How are you feeling, by the way?" Bilo asked as the shuttle skillfully was maneuvered around yet another turn to begin a descent along a ramp leading to another level.

"Truthfully?"

"Would you lie to a superior officer?" Bilo asked with a smile.

"Actually, I'm not quite sure I can describe just how I do feel," Renson said.

Which made Bilo chuckle.

"It's just the silax-capsule at work in your system," Bilo explained.

"I've been meaning to ask more about the purpose of the capsule," Renson said. "Do you suppose now would be just as good of a time as any?"

"It's merely a relaxant," Bilo said. "Really nothing too powerful, you understand. Given only because the General seems to think a mere Lieutenant might become a bit uptight and cowed in a social event consisting of superiors. Are you uptight and cowed by that prospect?"

"Not in the least."

"See," Bilo said, delivering a delighted laugh. "The silax-capsule is working its miracles already."

Renson liked Bilo. He really did like him. He continued to like him until they reached the Lyro-pod and the horrors of the interrogation began.

CHAPTER NINE

General Jarun Faralum delivered the euology, all the while thinking what a loss it had been for Lieutenant Carlylean to have been the one on board the space shuttle when it had malfunctioned and exploded between the Trigon and the cordon of empty alien spacecraft.

Why Lieutenant Carlylean, especially now that it had seemed verified that Renson was fitting in perfectly? Had there been any doubts remaining, after the part Renson had played in the interrogation around Tibur-I, that he had been one of them?

Damned rotten stroke of luck! And Jarun had said as much.

What in the hell had gone wrong to make the shuttle

just explode like that? Jarun had raised an uproar, calling in the Head Maintenance Officer and putting him on the carpet, only to get his insistence that the shuttle had been in A-1 working order when Renson had taken it out. And, if the Chief Maintenance Officer said it was in prime condition, there was little reason to doubt him, even if such a response would have been a natural one to save his skin. The officer had been with the Trigon for the past two missions, and Jarun had found him exceptionally competent during that time.

Yet, if the shuttle was in excellent flying condition, what had happened to it?

A counterattack offered by the enemy ships? That seemed hardly likely in that the shuttle was being monitored at the time, and there had been no visible firing from any of the enemy spacecraft, quite aside from the fact that the two spacecraft within firing range had already been determined to be disabled.

Very strange! All . . . very . . . very strange.

As if the death of Lieutenant Carlylean wasn't a mystery in itself, what was the purpose of this cordon of alien spacecraft strung out across this section of empty space? No one had yet explained that to Jarun's satisfaction, although he did have his suspicions.

The wall obviously had been designed by someone of high intelligence, someone, perhaps, surpassing the technical know-how of even the Kyralean Empire; although, they were obviously alien to anything now

136

existing within the Kyralean realm of influence. Nothing about them computed. Not their ship design, the construction materials, or anything else gleaned from a thorough search of the spacecraft. Certainly not their means of communication. If those broadcasts being continually beamed from the spacecraft were actually relaying some kind of intelligent message, it couldn't be decoded.

It was from this cordon of spacecraft, poised here on the brink of the deserted space beyond, that those messages had been coming that had for so long baffled the General and Lieutenant Carlylean. The latter having been the communications officer who had received them.

In fact, it had been Renson Carlylean's purpose to, one more time, see if he couldn't find something on board one of the disabled alien ships, something to help him in deciphering the broadcasts, which had sent him back one more time—to find nothing—to be blown to smithereens during his attempted return to the Trigon.

There were fifty alien ships altogether. Fifty of them stretched out in a long line. None of them, at least as far as Jarun could determine, was now being crewed by anything but automatic devices which triggered, among other things, a destruction beam (unidentified by the Trigon computer) each time a foreign object (like a spacecraft) drew within range. Even then, the beam seemed mostly programmed to

137

fire in warning, rather than directly at the craft.

What a shock it had been for Jarun to run onto something like this out in the middle of nowhere!

When the Trigon had originally approached to the point where the alien ships were finally being registered upon the viewer screen, indicated as the apparent source of the mysterious radio broadcasts, Jarun had thought they were lined up for battle. He had been very tempted to beat a retreat right there and then.

Except something had seemed strange even then. Like the way the ships kept to their positions, unmoving. Like the way they refused to answer Jarun's attempts at communicating with them, giving no response to his heralds except for more of the same undecipherable static the Trigon had been picking up sporadically for space-days.

Jarun, rather than retreat, had ordered a slower approach. Much as a mouse, sensing possible danger, but not really being sure of it, might approach a sleeping cat, Jarun had simply found the temptation too great to resist.

Continued attempts to open up channels of communication had failed, the alien cordon giving up nothing except a duplicate of the same static as before, accompanied by a bit more as reception improved with the narrowing of distance between alien spacecraft and ExploraStarShip Trigon.

Still, the Trigon computer failed to compute any apparent meaning to the broadcasts. Renson Carlylean, then still alive, had been unable to make heads or tails out of them, either.

Jarun had put the Trigon on battle alert and had approached it even closer to the alien cordon. All along, there had been no apparent signs of life on the other ships. The ships, in fact, looked as if they had been lined up in their present positions and then abandoned. In fact, Jarun had been just about to decide they were completely deserted when the Trigon had been fired upon. Or, rather, there had been an apparent warning shot fired across the Trigon's nose, exploding in a brilliant asterisk of blinding white light.

Jarun had ordered the Trigon stopped and had, then, requested a computer analysis of the alien weapon beam. The Trigon computer, though, had been unable to compute, as usual, anything whatsoever about the beam or the spacecraft which had fired it.

Continued attempts were made to contact the alien spacecraft, still without success. And, as long as the Trigon remained stationary, the alien spacecraft remained silent. However, the minute Jarun ordered a resumption of approach, another warning beam had been fired, bringing the Trigon to another standstill.

Was it then that Jarun had first begun to suspect that what he was facing was a protective wall that had been placed to keep out anyone who had come in search of the wealth of Zythin? What other purpose was there for this floating defensive wall, if not to keep out intruders? And, such fortifications weren't erected if there wasn't something to protect, were they?

No matter what indication being presently given that there was nothing beyond the wall but totally empty space, that might only have been an illusion. Jarun had found protecto-screens before which had masked whole planets. Therefore, there was the possibility of worlds existing within that apparent void, worlds unseen only because Jarun was being prevented from getting closer to them—in much the same way he had been unaware of these spacecraft until he had been able to come close enough to register their presence.

He ordered a shuttle craft launched toward the cordon, wanting to see just what would happen if warning shots weren't heeded. What he discovered was that, if warning shots weren't taken seriously, the beams were aimed directly at the oncoming target. The sacrificial shuttle had been dissolved, leaving nothing in its place. Not anything like the destruction of Lieutenant Carlylean's shuttle which had blown debris every which direction.

Jarun hadn't opened fire in retaliation, only because the computer aboard the Trigon still failed to give him an analysis of the enemy beam's makeup. Without knowing that, it was impossible to compute how the Trigon forcefields would stand up under the barrage which would most likely be returned if the Trigon did open fire.

Besides, the alien cordon made no move to fire directly at the Trigon as long as the ExploraShip indicated no apparent moves to continue further violation of guarded territory.

Jarun ordered the Trigon into a sideways slip, proceeding in a parallel path to the cordon, sliding by first one alien ship and then the other.

The alien spacecraft were all duplicates, one looking exactly like the other, as if cloned from the same metallic mother. All, that is, except for two of them.

"Looks as if someone got here before us," Sub-Commander Niltak had said as a closer magnification revealed that two ships in the line had obviously been damaged. Large stretches of melted metal scarred the ships' exteriors.

"What do you think?" Jarun asked. "Do you think there's a safe passage existing between the two?"

"Want to risk another shuttle to find out?" Bilo suggested.

Jarun sent in another shuttle which quickly proved there was, indeed, an existing breach in the enemy defenses. The shuttle reached as far as one of the damaged ships without drawing any fire.

Jarun found the results conducive to conflicting emotions. If there was a breach in the cordon, that meant the Trigon could possibly squeeze through to the other side without sustaining damages. On the other hand, if the Trigon could do it now, that meant some other ship could have done exactly the same thing in the past. And, if that had been the case, there was the distinct possibility that someone had gotten to the wealth of the Cities of Zythin before them.

Not that Jarun was aware of any other raiders operating in deep space. He knew that there had probably never been any under the charter of the High Commander of Kyrale which had ventured this far. That didn't, however, mean that somewhere, out there in the wide universe, there weren't creatures with high intelligence ratios who had the lust for conquest which Jarun and his men possessed.

Jarun boarded the disabled enemy ships, finding fully automated life-support systems that still (despite the damage) continued to operate and supply a breathable atmosphere.

The ships, also, contained skeletons of humanoidal creatures, the skeletons scattered through the ships to such an extent that it would have appeared they had not been killed by whatever it was that had damaged the ships' exteriors.

Large solariums, still sprouting forests of greenery which were tended by robots, existed. The robots silently continued their programmed chores, despite the sudden introduction of Kyraleans into their midst. Trees and shrubs were so bounteous with edible fruit and nuts, it seemed hardly likely the previous occupants had perished from starvation.

One of Jarun's men found a pile of sketches in one of the apparent control rooms (though, no one aboard the

Trigon even the Chief Maintenance Engineer, brought over for the purpose, could make sense of any of the control equipment).

"Zythineans!" Jarun exclaimed, looking at some figures sketched on a material that resembled Kyralean plasto-paper but which was composed of some entirely different molecular structure.

The sketches showed creatures of large bodies, covered from head to foot with long, silky hair, having three massive arms, having three eyes and two noses.

"I would say there is little doubt but that the Zythineans passed this way," Bilo agreed. "No doubt at all, from the evidence. And, since the skeletons aboard would tend to indicate the crew of these particular ships were humanoid, I would say the sketches record the passing of the Zythineans and not their taking over these spacecraft."

"Maybe they even caused the damage when they crashed through the cordon?" Jarun suggested.

"There's always that possibility, to be certain," Bilo agreed.

"The Trigon had stayed in place for seven space days, because an examination of the disabled spaceships (approach to the fully operational ones continuing to remain impossible) provided an interesting diversion.

Lieutenant Carlylean had, also, had hopes of finding some clue to the alien communications which would have allowed him a means of decoding the broadcasts which continued to be automatically transmitted from not one but several of the alien craft.

Up until the end, though, the ships had remained a total mystery. No one could figure out how they were powered, of what material they were constructed, where they had come from, what they were doing lined up in space where they were. . . .

When Jarun had sensed the interest of his crew waning, he had decided it was time to move on. The attraction, after all, that the spacecrafts would have obviously held out for scientists over a longer period of time couldn't be expected to keep the interest of men who had come into deep space in search of treasure and more exotic forms of amusement.

There seemed to be very little on board the ships that could pass for something of recognizable value. The chance for any amusement offered by interrogations of the alien crew had been negated by the deaths of all native populations on board.

Jarun had been readying the Trigon for the continuation of their journey in search of the Zythinean Cities, constructed by creatures who had obviously passed this way, when Lieutenant Carlylean had put in his request to journey one more time to the disabled alien ships in an attempt to find something that might allow his putting some meaning to the automatic broadcasts. Jarun had given permission.

Mistake! Mistake! But, how was he to have known that something was going to go wrong within the mechanical guts of the shuttle, sending it and its pilot to space-dust? Although, Jarun supposed he could be thankful Lieutenant Carlylean had been the only passenger at the time of the disaster.

"Thinking about Lieutenant Carlylean?" Sub-Commander Niltak asked, joining his friend at one of the observation windows.

"You guessed that, did you?"

"He did have that air of innocence about him that was as exciting as all hell, didn't he?" Bilo asked, although it was more of a statement. He gave a sigh of nostalgia. "So unlike those who are so thoroughly jaded before they reach us."

"He was fitting in, wasn't he, Bilo?" Jarun asked.

"You had your doubts?" Bilo asked curiously. "After having been there for the interrogation of the Tiburians?"

"He was under the influence of a silex-capsule at the time, wasn't he?" Jarun reminded.

"You and I both know that silax will eliminate certain inhibitions, but hardly to the point of Renson's response."

"But we don't know that for sure, do we? Silax reacts on individual systems differently. Even if it were true that the silax had nothing whatsoever to do with it, some people often can't adjust to a peek given at the other side of their psyches, can they?"

"Meaning you think Lieutenant Carlylean wasn't as well-adjusted as he seemed? Faking it, you suggest?"

He laughed in response to the assumed absurdity of his question.

"He was doing some pretty good faking if he fooled me," Bilo said finally.

"He did have you convinced, then?"

"He was already beginning to sample the C-Series in the pleaso-cylinders. Does that sound like someone who wasn't a little hooked?"

"The shuttle had received a full inspection two days before it destructed," Jarun said. "I can't believe the mechanics couldn't have spotted the possibility of a malfunction great enough to blow the shuttle and its passenger into a thousand pieces."

"You're insinuating suicide?"

"I suppose there is little point in insinuating anything at this point of the game, is there?" Jarun said.

"Point well taken!" Bilo agreed. "All water under the bridge, yes?"

"And, once again, the Trigon seems to be without a communications officer. We seem to be pretty rough on them, don't we?"

"Corporal Porscion seems capable enough," Bilo observed. "Not too much is demanded by a communications officer in this part of space, anyway, is there? Not too many occupants of these alien spacecraft seem to be interested in doing too much talking."

"So, I suppose it's time to put it all behind us and move on, yes?"

"Yes."

"There are, after all, worlds out there waiting to be sacked, are there not?"

"Ten cities in particular."

"Yes, ten fabulous cities," Jarun said, turning slightly so he was looking out over one of the disabled alien ships.

Bilo followed Jarun's gaze.

"Looks completely empty out there, doesn't it?" Jarun said. "Not a star, not a planet in sight."

"Suspiciously empty, wouldn't you agree?" Bilo said. "It might be explainable if there was evidence of a black hole out there, but there is no sign of evident turmoil. No sign at all."

"Complete with a wall of alien spacecraft automatically protecting the area from invasion. Seems a mighty powerful line of defense constructed to protect nothing, doesn't it?"

"We might be dealing with protecto-screens, yes?"

"Why not?"

"If a bit of technology a mite sophisticated for the primitives we might have hoped to be confronting."

"We're not exactly unprepared, are we?" Jarun reminded.

"And, as an official ambassador of the Kyralean Empire, you can always claim diplomatic reasons for moving us in closer to observe any defenses. That is the whole purpose of the charter from The High Commander, isn't it?"

"Of course," Jarun said.

"But something continues to bother you?"

"Yes, and I don't know what," Jarun said. "I don't like the feeling either. It's something I don't recall ever having felt before."

"You'll be feeling differently once we're on the move again," Bilo promised. "This, after all, is a graveyard we're sitting on here, isn't it? Oh, that battle line operates, but only because of mechanical intricacies we can't understand. The men behind those machines are long gone. Converted to skeletons by what, huh? Now that the novelty of this part of space has worn off, I figure the men are ready to move on. I know I am. Lieutenant Carlylean, after all, was a popular member of the crew, and sticking around only keeps his tragedy freshly in mind."

So they moved the next day, maneuvering the ExploraStarShips through the space that would have been protected by the crossfire from two alien spacecraft if those two spacecraft hadn't been previously disabled.

Tautly drawn nerves were almost set off when the Danner-D apparently moved too far in one flanking movement, causing an alien craft, next down the line, to fire off a beam that came up short of doing any real damage.

Once safely on the other side of the cordon, Jarun brought the ExploraStarShips to a stop one more time for yet another complete check of the computer systems. As they would soon be moving in a section of space offering no stars or planets on which to trinagulate position, it was going to be the job of the computer to get them out once they entered.

Jarun then ordered the ships forward, sensors scanning in an attempt to detect protecto-screens which kept solid masses momentarily masked from view. All, however, that was immediately registered was empty space.

So complete was the blackness they entered, as a matter of fact, it was impossible to tell by looking out any of the observation windows,, whether they were moving at all. Time was noted by the automatic registering of lighting that brightened and dimmed according to the computer-determined progression of any given space-day. And in those areas of the spacecraft where bright light was necessitated on an around-the-clock basis, such as on the Control Deck, crew members checked the various digital readouts to find out the hour.

It was 1400 hours according to the digital readout on the main computer board on the Trigon Control Deck, when General Jarun Faralum, Commander-General of the ExploraStarShips Trigon, Danner-D, and Kyronal-IV, sitting in the control seat, noticed the strange blue glow that was suddenly beginning to diffuse the room.

"Bilo?" Jarun asked, turning the control chair to face the Sub-Commander who was sitting but a few feet away.

"What in the hell. . . ?" Bilo replied. That being the last recorded words of a crew member of the ExploraStarShip Trigon before all on board it and its sister-ships died.

EPILOGUE

They had all been women!
Women!
Did he believe it?

Maybe he had made another mistake. He had made mistakes before. Many . . . many mistakes over the last two-hundred tirem.

Anyway, he assumed it had been two-hundred tirem. Two-hundred-twenty-seven per his present computations. Although, admittedly, his computations weren't one-hundred percent accurate, were they? There were days when he forgot things, forgot to record the passing of a space-day or two.

How many space-days had he forgotten altogether?
On the other hand, what difference did it make?

He glanced back at the paper in front of him. He bent close to it, because his eyes weren't what they had once been.

Women!

He read again, carefully, taking extreme pains to transcribe each letter according to the code he had attributed to it.

Had he actually succeeded? Had he actually—finally—deciphered this foreign language, made it possible to unlock the mysteries of this place? Mysteries which had for so many tirem escaped him, only because he couldn't decipher any data at his fingertips?

He had thought he would die before the secret was his, hadn't he? Oh, once he had imagined that the ExploraStarShips Trigon, Danner-D, or Kyronal-IV would be back for him, picking him up on their return to Kyrale. Renson even had a story for them to explain how he had managed to survive the explosion of the space shuttle. Although at the moment he wasn't quite sure just what the story had been going to be. His memory, like his eyesight, wasn't like it had once been.

Of what importance would have been that lie anymore, anyway, since, had the Exploraships been going to return, they would have surely come back this way long before now.

So, what had happened to General Jarun, Sub-Commander Niltak, Ricky, Maxwell, Lxic? Were they actually still alive out there? Or had he managed to outlive them?

Strange, but he figured he should have been dead by now. He had figured the same disease which had wiped out the alien humanoids might return eventually to wipe him out, too.

But if the aliens had been women, he needn't necessarily have feared. Women, exposed for long periods of time to deep space, were susceptible to *micomanifolicsis*, weren't they? These alien women had been destroyed by the same disease that had wiped out Kyralean women, forcing the High Command to disallow any women on ExploraShip crews.

Anyway, even if the aliens hadn't called the disease the same, their term being simply *donof*, then the symptoms were the same, weren't they?

Renson hurried on with his translation. He was hungry to know. If only he could have broken the code tirem ago, he would have had time to know so much more. But time for him was running out. A man, being a social animal, didn't manage in complete isolation all that well. There were times when Renson had thoughts he would be far better off dead.

He consciously cast such morbid thoughts from his mind, hurrying on in his anxiousness to translate the mysteries.

They had been women from the Planet Nexel, which—at least, at the moment—Renson hadn't the foggiest notion where it might be located within the galaxy. They had been part of a volunteer group which had left Nexel to come here and set up this line.

But set it up, why? Renson couldn't seem to find out why. The secret was undoubtedly buried in the piles of paperwork he had been able to scrounge up over the tirem. Or, maybe, the secrets weren't here but locked away on one of the other alien spacecraft to which he still didn't have access. Wouldn't that have been the final irony?

But then, his life had been full of irony, hadn't it?

It had been ironic that the event which had convinced everyone—even General Faralum—that Renson was a firm member of the Trigon crew, had turned out to be the same event that had convinced Renson he would have to abandon ship.

That event being his participation in the interrogation of Tiburian primitives in the Lyro-pod Ram.

His desertion was not a decision Renson had made lightly, considering he had been born and raised for military service. Yet after the interrogation, it was an action Renson knew he would have to take if he wished to preserve a certain part of his sanity which was virtually on the point of collapse.

There was no way Renson could imagine himself traveling with the ship to the completion of its journey, and back again to Kyrale, and doing so in mental safety. Oh, his body might have survived, but his mind would have never made it.

What was going on aboard the ExploraStarShip Trigon was a mind-bender far more intense and enduring than anything experienced in a pleaso-cylinder, no matter how advanced the index code related when the request for such was whispered sultrily into the ear.

What, of course, had scared Renson the most wasn't the fact that all of those primitives had so horribly been put to death, nor that he had helped in their execution. Although both of those aspects of the interrogation had been enough to scare Renson plenty. But the most frightening thing of all—the most frightening thing by far—was the point wherein it struck Renson that he was actually (amid all of the horror and revulsion) beginning to enjoy what was happening.

Enjoyment: that was the ultimate horror.

Some say it is an acquired taste. Well, it frightened Renson no end that it just might have been a taste he could acquire by the journey's end. And it was one he didn't want to acquire.

Oh, it might have been one thing if, like everyone else aboard the spacecraft, he had been born with such twisted inner needs. Then, being assigned to the Trigon would have had its advantages, in that it would have allowed him an escape from a civilization which would have been formally frightened by his inner savagery. The excursions, then, into deep space would have allowed him the catharsis which would have cleansed him, pulled the dangerous fuse, so to speak, so that he might have operated as a "normal" human being during his brief returns to the civilized world. In that way, the killing of the primitives might even have been rationalized, in that their deaths helped maintain the sanity of men who probably had far more to contribute than the primitives ever did.

However, to take a man like Renson, normal by all civilized standards, and attempt to distort him into something that wasn't the accepted norm, was perversion beyond belief! By doing so, it made a normal human being a sexual outlaw, someone who could no longer function within a civilized society because primitive needs (long tempered by civilizing influences) had once again been called to the surface, doubtfully ever to be pushed back into their protective caverns within.

He had actually enjoyed his part in the interrogation. He had actually achieved a certain sexual high which—while obviously not as pronounced as that had by either General Faralum or Sub-Commander Niltak—had still been lurking there beneath Renson's distaste and nausea.

And while it would have been very easy to blame what had happened on the silax-capsule he had taken—there was, after all, no mention of the drug silex in any of the medio-memory-banks of the computer—Renson had refused to accept the fact that there was any drug that could have so completely allowed for his reversion to the primitive. And, if there was such a drug, people like General Faralum and

Sub-Commander Niltak having access to it, then, that was even more of a reason for Renson to have plotted getting away.

The question had become, of course, not only how to get away but where to get away to. Renson had been way beyond the Kyralean realm of influence when he had made his fateful decision. He had been deep in space, beyond Tibur-I, speeding through Scalic Area III.

The alien blockade, once it had been determined it was vacant, had offered Renson a solution to most of his problems. It had a breathable atmosphere. It had a constant food supply. It offered protection. It was located on the route the ExploraShips could be expected to take on their return, since the very nature of the space was that the ship computer would be expected to backtrack along the pathway the ship had used upon entering, much as if a thread had been trailed to assure safe escape. That being the case, Renson wouldn't be trapped out in the middle of nowhere. Coming up with a tale of his survival, despite the exploded shuttle craft, would have had him welcomed back aboard the returning spacecraft. Then, once the ship once again reached Kyrale, Renson would have moved for a transfer.

He, of course, had exploded the shuttle, using automatic radio waves, while hidden in a position of safety aboard the alien craft. He had remained hidden until the Exploraships had moved on and left him.

Never . . . to . . . come . . . back!

Renson had occupied his time in trying to translate the alien language, having had no success until now.

Now he was finally able to get some inkling as to why this place was here. This place that had become simultaneously his salvation and his prison.

It was here because a volunteer group of Nexelians (were all Nexelians women?) had come to this place to deposit. . . .

Deposit what? Renson searched for the answer, but he couldn't immediately come up with the consecutive paperwork. He moved on to what was available.

They had been attacked by spaceships, apparently from Zythin, by the descriptions and pictures drawn of the attacking forces. The Nexelians had tried to warn the Zythineans. . . .

Warn them regarding what?

. . .But, the warning, because of a failure in communication, wasn't understood or heeded.

The Zythineans had broken through, leaving the Nexelian defenses breached. The breach would have been repaired, but the Nexelians had suddenly been struck down by *donof* and had begun dying.

Renson quit reading, realizing he could sift through reams of paper and still never find the answer to all his questions. On the other hand, his breaking of the language code did give him the key he needed for a possible quicker answering of his questions. Because, if the Nexelians had tried to warn the unheeding

Zythineans, then, it could be suspected the Nexelian equipment had been programmed to warn off all approaching spacecraft, the Kyralean ExploraStarShips included.

The secrets, then, might very well be succinctly spelled out within the radio broadcasts still being constantly transmitted from the alien spacecraft strung out to either side of the two disabled ones Renson was using.

He got up, taking hallways which had long become familiar. He knew where he was going. As a communications officer, it had been the radio equipment which had gotten his first attention—back in those days when he had never dreamed he would be here for over two-hundred tirem.

He reached the Control Room, hurriedly crossing to the radio console and the computer plug-ins.

Three hours later he was ready, activating audio.

"You are being forewarned!" a metallic voice began, making it obvious that further adjustments would be necessary to make the verbal crystal clear. "You are presently on a flight path that will bring you into an area being used as a dump for waste material arising as a by-product of fisorial reaction. . . ."

What, Renson wondered, was fisorial reaction?

". . .and, thus, must be considered highly dangerous. You are therefore instructed, for your own safety, to please re-route accordingly, detouring via coordinates 2/4/6542 or 2/6/4493."

Renson turned up the volume.

"THIS SPACE IS CONDEMNED as dangerous to all known lifeforms. Repeat: THIS SPACE IS CONDEMNED. . . ."

THE END